ELE

AND

BINDWEED

A collection of
short stories by
Phil Lawder

ISBN: 978-1-9997129-4-5

Cover design by Colin Robinson

Introduction

Over the last few years, ideas for short stories have pinged into my head. When the demon work has not got in the way, I have eased or forced them onto paper, and there they have lain, occasionally shared at open mics and writing groups.

Some come out sad, even tragic, some wistful, some funny. I guess that just depends on my mood at the time. I've deliberately mixed them up in the book.

One benefit of lockdown's forced incarceration has been the elimination of alibis, reasons not to get on with reviewing, rewriting and gathering them together.

So, here they are. I hope that you find something to fit your mood.

Phil

CONTENTS

John's Interesting Sunday	7
Two Down	17
The Flow and the Ebb of the Tide	27
A Good Night Out	33
Rain, Swings and Things You Don't Talk About	39
The Sculptor	43
Midnight	49
Princess	51
The Daily Sudoku	61
Plum	65
Anthony Hawkins	71
The Visitation	73
Craggy Face	77
Marjorie's Garden	81

England Expects 87

Starlight 91

A Bowl of Cherries 97

Summer with Ellie 105

Elephants and Bindweed 111

JOHN'S INTERESTING SUNDAY

The day after John and Charlotte had sex in the Architectural Ceramics Room of the Victoria and Albert Museum, it rained. Not that John noticed. That morning, he could have been walking through thunder, lightning and hail and the grin would still have been fixed to his face.

'Waterman,' his boss barked at him around half past ten. 'Did you leave that sparkling brain of yours at home today? I expect great things of you but instead I find you gazing out of the window like a sloth on Valium. Pull yourself together, man, and straighten your tie. This is the Ministry of Defence, not some hippy advertising agency.'

John tried very hard to concentrate. He was good at his job – five years out of university, a PhD in Metallurgy and regarded as one of the department's top experts in the dynamics of torpedoes. But this morning, every time he thought of torpedoes, he started to giggle. He poured himself another coffee, stared at his screen with a look that he hoped was of deep concentration; his fingers hovered over the keyboard, waggling like an empty-handed puppeteer. But every time he edged towards present reality, images of the previous afternoon swept him back.

Like all of his life, John's Sundays ran to a tidy pattern. Ten o'clock church with his parents, to sing hearty hymns and drink thin coffee, nodding along to the racism and detailed aches and pains of the elderly congregation. Then a full roast lunch, always preceded by his father proclaiming 'Ah, the fine roast beef of old England', even if it was pork or lamb. In the afternoon while his parents snoozed, John would play World of Warcraft. After a precious two hours, his mother, refreshed and recharged, would tell him that staring at a screen for so long would make him blind and she couldn't understand why he was sitting inside on such a sunny day. A long walk was always deemed a suitable penance. He would take the permanently scowling family Yorkie round the ornamental gardens in the centre of their tidy suburb, pooper scooper in hand. The rest of the day passed in eating, watching television and ensuring that he had a clean shirt for Monday morning.

This Sunday, however, had been different. A life-long fascination with Samurai warriors had drawn him to an exhibition of costumes at the V&A, on loan from the Tokyo National Museum and shortly to close. His announcement that he was heading off after lunch brought a heavily laden 'Oh' from his parents, followed, as he tried to explain, by 'No, no, that's fine. You get on and enjoy yourself. We'll be… fine.'

And so, at half past three that Sunday, John found himself in the great vaulted foyer of the V&A, clutching his ticket in eager anticipation. He was about halfway round the exhibition, carefully reading each description and jotting down notes in the small red notebook that he always carried. Then his life changed quite fundamentally.

The problem with public exhibitions is that the public are there. John would have much preferred a solitary wander at his own speed. He was particularly irritated by a couple in their early twenties who seemed to be keeping pace with him. Thinking back afterwards, John found that he couldn't remember the man particularly well. Tall, casually dressed, longish hair. That was about it. The girl was much more striking. Red hair that curled around her face, enormous eyes and that very pale skin that real redheads have. She was dressed all in black, in a jumper and short skirt and long boots that came up to her knees.

They clearly had been arguing all day and had brought the argument with them into the exhibition. John guessed that they were the kind that quite enjoyed an audience. Whatever the man said about an exhibit would be greeted by her with a dismissive 'Well, you would say that, wouldn't you' or 'I suppose *she'd* agree with you about that', all delivered with a slight Midlands twang, that set John's teeth on edge.

Things came to a head as they stood in front of the main exhibit, a particularly fine set of o-yoroi armour from the twelfth-century Heian period. This was the piece that John had been looking forward to most. Despite his best efforts, the couple were now standing beside him. They all studied the piece in silence. Then the girl spun round abruptly and stared at John. He tried to ignore her and concentrate on the soft lustre of the armour, but there was something about the intensity of her stare. Eventually, he could not help but glance towards her.

'You're a man,' she announced. John struggled to think of a reply to this rather obvious observation. He settled for a shrug and turned back to the exhibit. She was not to be deterred so easily.

'Tell me, are all men complete bastards or is it just this one?' The voice had quietened, though the anger clearly hadn't.

John prided himself on the power of his logic. And so, despite wanting to stay uninvolved, he couldn't resist pointing out the fallacy in her question.

'I think you'll find that there's a large gap between the particular and the general in this case, by which I mean that the two options that you put forward are not the only options. The most likely scenario is, in fact, that some men are, as you say, bastards, as indeed are some women.'

He turned back to the armour, hoping that this would end the discussion. He was wrong. If anything, her stare intensified.

'That's brilliant!' she exclaimed and, turning to her companion, 'So, I suggest that you crawl back to wherever bastards fester and sod off out of my life.'

'You know,' responded her companion, 'I might just do that,' and marched out of the room.

John, aware that others were watching, felt that now would be a good time to clear his throat and move on to the next exhibit. He was stopped by what sounded like a gasp and then a sob from the girl next to him. John's experience with girls up to this point had established that they were, as a species, impossible to understand, communicate with or console, so he began to edge away. Then he felt an arm loop through his.

'I'm sorry,' she whispered in a much-subdued voice. 'It's just that I thought, you know, that he was someone special. And then he goes and ...'

The voice trailed off. John considered his options and settled for nodding, slowly.

'Listen,' she continued, tightening her grip. 'Would it be too much to ask for you to take me for a coffee? It's just that I'm a bit wobbly after all that, you know.'

John was in uncharted waters. Without any semblance of a paddle. He stared around, concerned about how much of the exhibition he would miss if he went off with this strange woman. Realising that he was, in fact, nearly at the end, a faint excitement grew in him. An actual woman was asking him to go and have coffee with her.

'I'll pay, if that's what's bothering you,' she added. John glanced at her and thought he detected a faint smile below the glistening eyes.

'No, no, it's not that, it's just… I'm … I was thinking, wondering …'

'I think the exit's over there. Come on.' And she pulled at his arm.

They sat in the domed coffee area at the back of the museum, squeezed into a table that she chose at the back. She spooned up some froth from her cappuccino, licked it in a way that John found charming and worryingly erotic, and told him her tale. She was Charlotte, newly arrived in London to join her boyfriend, Paul, the one who had stormed off, and working at a gallery in Dover Street as a receptionist until something more interesting came up. And, of course, now discovering that Paul had got impatient in her absence and had been spreading his favours around. John found that, now he was listening to the cadence of her voice rather than the words, the accent was no longer irritating. A realisation that she had stopped talking and was looking at him expectantly caught him by surprise.

'Sorry, what was that last bit?'

'I was asking what you thought of the exhibition.'

Seizing his moment, John gave a full and detailed description of the history of samurai armour from the eleventh century to the eighteenth. She listened with a wide-eyed gaze and slightly open mouth, occasionally brushing her red hair from her face. John was used to his listener's attention drifting into glazed-eyed disinterest within a couple of minutes and was astonished and grateful that

Charlotte remained apparently transfixed. Nevertheless, he paused after six or seven minutes.

'Look, I must be boring you,' he said, looking fearfully for signs of agreement.

'Not at all, it's so rare to find someone who really knows his subject rather than the usual bullshitters.' John was still having trouble hearing such words from such a beautiful mouth but tried not to show it. 'Tell you what, though, let's give your voice a rest. I'll show you my favourite room in this museum. Come on.'

She stood up and reached out to him. John discreetly rubbed his palm down the side of his trousers to get rid of the sweat that had sprung up. He took the proffered hand and allowed himself to be dragged along to the stairs and up to the top floor room.

Charlotte stood in the doorway and flung her arms wide.

'The Architectural Ceramics Room,' she announced. 'Isn't this the most amazing space?'

John looked around. Panels and cabinets displayed brightly coloured ceramics from across the centuries and around the world, all gleaming and glistening under the bright lights. There was certainly an air of magic.

'I've never been up here before,' he admitted.

'That's what so great. No one ever comes up here. Even the guard is usually off having a fag or whatever. You could walk around naked if you wanted to.'

The image lodged itself firmly in John's mind and would not go away. He didn't want it to go away.

John found it difficult afterwards to remember the exact sequence of events. As far as he could work out, one minute Charlotte was telling him about the detail on some fourteenth-century Persian tiles; then she was kissing him and telling him she had never met anyone like him; then, shortly afterwards, they were behind one of the exhibition panels, his trousers were round his ankles – he was eternally grateful that he hadn't worn his Superman underpants – and he had a grin on his face that had not yet departed.

The call came on Monday at about half past eleven. He had given Charlotte his number more in hope than expectation; good things rarely happened once, let alone twice, in John's life.

'Hi John, Charlotte. Fancy meeting for a sandwich?' Her voice sounded brisk, which John put down to her being at work. 'About one, at Pret in the Strand?'

'Sounds great. I'll see you there.'

The rest of the morning was no more productive. At five to one he was outside Pret. At five past, an agonising ten minutes later, she appeared.

'Hi.' She gave him a peck on the cheek. 'Look, the rain's cleared. Let's grab something and go and sit by the river.'

On a bench in the Embankment Gardens, looking across the Thames to the monumental slabs of the South Bank, John bit into his cheese and tomato sandwich. This felt right, sitting here with a girl, his girl, he dared to think, enjoying some together time.

'Can I just say,' he ventured, 'yesterday was fantastic. I mean, never in my life….'

'Yes,' Charlotte cut in. 'About yesterday. There's something I have to tell you.'

John felt a crunch in the pit of his stomach. He put his sandwich down carefully on the bench.

'What?'

'You probably didn't notice but there's a gallery that runs round the top of that room.'

'Can't say I did.'

'Well, there is, and the fact is…' she hesitated. 'Well, Paul was up there. And, well, he took these.'

She reached into her bag, drew out a set of photos and handed them to him. John glanced at them and dropped them on the bench as if they were red hot.

'Gosh,' he muttered.

'Well, yes, as you say, gosh.'

'But this must be terribly embarrassing for you.'

'Not really.'

'What do you mean?'

'Well, you see, John, I knew he was there.'

John stared at her. His mouth opened but no words formed. She put her hand on his.

'John, I'm a bit of an exhibitionist, as you may have noticed. But there is something else.'

John tried to remember how to breathe.

'You see,' Charlotte continued, 'you're getting quite famous, in a very, what can I say, exclusive circle. MoD high-flyer, expert in torpedoes, guidance systems, propellants, all that sort of thing.'

John was falling down a very deep hole. The world around him blackened. He gripped the bench, gripping reality.

'The thing is, John, there are people who are very interested in you and your clever brain. They would love to meet you and talk, you know, hear about what you're working on.'

John managed to shake his head.

'Yes, John, I can understand how that might not seem to be a good thing. But surely, it must be better than these photos getting out. You do see my point, don't you?'

John did see her point. He imagined the reaction of his parents, the people at church, the office colleagues who called him the departmental nerd. Everyone who, for so long, had defined who he should be. And light dawned. In a moment of translucent clarity, he saw his new future. He understood what he had to do.

He stood up. 'Charlotte, and I appreciate that's probably not your name, of course, I'd like you to do something for me. I'd like you to send these photos to everyone I know. I'll send you a list of contacts. Mind you, given that you knew I would be at the museum yesterday means you've hacked me, so I suppose you've already got them. Meanwhile, I'll take these.'

He reached down and gathered up the pile of prints from the bench.

'I'll leave you the sandwich. And, Charlotte, thank you.'

It was her turn to be speechless.

John walked back to the Ministry clutching his photos. The smile, though now slightly lopsided, was still on his face.

2 DOWN

The pen hovered over the paper.

'2 down. Soft warm glow on the meadow at Jane's hero's home. Nine letters.'

George looked out of the train window at the rows of identical houses flashing by. He tapped his biro against his teeth.

'Soft. That's usually a p. And that fits with one across. Warm glow? Satisfaction, contentment, not sure about that.' George's muttering was just loud enough to disturb his neighbours. 'And who on earth is Jane?' Deep in thought, he straightened the index finger of his right hand and inserted it carefully into his right nostril, rotating as it went in.

Sitting opposite George, his wife Mary looked at him impassively, then returned to her book. Was it the fifth or sixth time that she had read *Pride and Prejudice*? The creased and grubby pages were like old friends, picking up a conversation where it had been left off years before. Laconic Mr Bennet, haughty Mr Darcy and her favourite, the thoroughly nice Mr Bingley were more real to her than many of the casual acquaintances that life in a small, dull market town put in her path. Sometimes she even preferred their company to that of George. In fact, she nearly always preferred their company to that of George. She turned away and gazed out of the window. The houses had briefly given way to farmland. Spring was bringing back some hesitant colour to the sodden earth and the dark trees.

For a moment, the sun struggled through the high-piled clouds, as a pond, surrounded by trees, flashed by. In that instant, Mary's thoughts were overwhelmed by the television image of Darcy plunging through the murky, sunlit water outside his mansion and emerging, sodden, all social veneer stripped away. Colin Firth glowered before her.

She sighed and closed her eyes. If it had been her standing on that sunlit terrace in front of the magnificent house and Darcy had approached her, dripping from the pond and burning with ardour, what would she have done? Would she have swooned into his arms? No, she knew herself too well. There was no escaping it, she would almost certainly have told him to keep his hands to himself and not to get her beautiful summer dress all dirty. Just as she knew that common sense would not have allowed her to follow Lydia's path, eloping with the wicked Mr Wickham. No, dear safe Mr Bingley was her choice. She wondered what that said about her and feared that she already knew.

Her mind went back, as it so often did nowadays, to that day, forty-six years ago, when she and George had married. The tall, handsome naval officer and his slim bride, captured forever in the silver frame on top of their television. They had taken a train journey that day too, happily speeding towards a honeymoon in Torquay and a new shared future. In the era of long-haired hippies and floaty clothes, they had seemed an incongruous couple. George's short hair and upright bearing and she in her smart new two-piece clearly signalled that they did not subscribe to the doctrine of free love and letting it all hang out. And when they danced, as they so often did then, it was swirling waltzes and hearty foxtrots, not the shapeless shakings of modern so-called dancing. Swirling in the arms of her handsome man, she had felt herself close to the magic of Jane Austen's Regency world.

That time, on the train, they had sat side by side; they had even shared the crossword. Now they were just another invisible aging couple as they headed for London, to see what could be salvaged from the dust of a stale love. Her Mr Bingley had grown old and dull.

George's finger withdrew, its work completed, and disappeared into his pocket. 'Back to 2 down.' he muttered. 'Got p, something warm, meadow, could be field or, what's that word, yes, lea. Sounds like a place name.' He moved on to other clues, his biro clicking triumphantly as he wrote in the answers. But Jane's dream home did not reveal itself.

He raised his head and looked out at the clouds towering over the land. They were of that almost solid quality that he had so enjoyed when at sea. Even as a child he had loved them, feeling that he could run across them, leaping from one peak to another, chasing the sun and free from earthbound worries. He smiled as, in his mind, he ranged across the skies. His spirit lifted and, for a moment, he was able to forget their destination, the cramped room with its tatty sofa that left them a foot lower than the counsellor, all condescending smiles and endless nods of understanding.

'What's the joke?' Mary's voice cut in.

'Oh, er, nothing, just something I read in the paper.' Embarrassed, he returned to his crossword. 'Bloody fool,' he thought. 'Why couldn't you have told her? What are you afraid of?' He looked across, searching for the vivacious girl that he had married so long ago, the girl who had run barefoot on the beach at Torquay and laughed as the raucous seagulls swooped. He drew breath to speak to her, but she had returned to that damn book again and the moment had passed. He shifted round in the seat, carefully positioning the paper so that he could look over it, without being noticed, at the girl across the aisle. Her straining blouse and tight jeans offered any number of promises, though none intended for him.

George was secretly rather pleased with his imagination, whether it be focused on cloud-jumping or the pornographic possibilities of fellow passengers. Somehow, though, it had seemed inappropriate to the way of life that had settled on him. The Navy had been about obeying orders and keeping everything tidy and, when the arrival of children had demanded his presence at home, he had put in thirty years with the Ministry of Defence, where imagination was positively frowned on. So, it had become a secret thing, kept in his head as a private world where he could cavort unobserved, even, increasingly, by Mary, who had pulled back from any flights of fantasy.

Mary looked up and glanced across at George. God, he was so unsubtle. Did he really think that anyone would be fooled? If she had been the girl that he was ogling so obviously, she would have slapped his face. Mind you, when had he last ogled her? Well, at least it showed that there was still a glimmer of interest. Perhaps these visits to London would have a happy ending.

She could not help but think of the first meeting last week with Miss Faversham. 'Faversham, rather than Havisham, though we do have, ha, ha, great expectations for our clients,' the large, comfortable lady had said and Mary had felt pleased that she recognised the reference. It had been her idea to go, of course, finally finding the dull silence of their marriage too stifling. George would never have come up with it, wouldn't even admit that anything was wrong. It had taken weeks to persuade him, as he pooh-

poohed any idea of some 'do-gooder Nosy Parker prying into our lives'. Finally, only an ultimatum of 'We do it or I leave' had bought him to heel, on condition that it was in London, where no one would know them and it was at midday, so they could get a cheap day return.

The meeting had not been totally successful, but they had made some progress. Miss Faversham had shown herself to be much more clever than expected, forcing George out of his non-committal grunts into fuller answers by a blend of teasing, sympathising and probing. Eventually, George had admitted that their relationship (a word that she knew he hated) was 'perhaps a bit off the boil'. He had then suddenly started to talk about the old days and something about running through the clouds together, which she had not really understood. But that seemed to embarrass him, and he had clammed up and stared out of the window. Still, it had got things started and he had agreed to another meeting.

Mary was not looking forward to this session; they had been given a task to complete during the week. She had listened with embarrassment as Miss Faversham instructed them to 'get to know each other again as individuals'. They were supposed to stroke each other's backs for five minutes each night. There had been an immediate silent agreement between them both not even to discuss this, let alone try it. Mary now felt like a third-former again, desperately concocting excuses for why the homework had not been done.

George put his paper down and turned again to look at the clouds. The train was now rushing through the outer suburbs of London, past giant DIY sheds and furniture warehouses but the clouds were undiminished. If he were to go dancing across them again today, whom would he want with him? The girl opposite? To his surprise, he realised that Mary would be the only one that he would want. Mary, with her slightly disapproving look and oh-so-tidy hair and her caution would still be his ideal partner.

He leaned forward and tapped her on the knee. She looked up, surprised, peering over her glasses at him.

'Mary,' he started hesitantly, 'Mary, there's something I need to, well, want to tell you.'

'What, can't it wait?' Mary glanced around, nervously aware of the other passengers.

'Well, OK, I suppose that it could wait. I mean, well, no, actually, it can't. It's about those clouds, you see.'

'Clouds again. What is it about you and clouds?'

George felt his heart sink. What was the point? She would not understand. But he now felt a desperate, urgent need to explain, to involve her in his world. He leaned closer to try one last time.

'You see, Mary, I've always had this idea that…'

At that moment there was a tremendous bang and their carriage lurched sideways. Lights went out. The ordered world became shapeless chaos. They were falling, tumbling. He reached for Mary but made no contact. He looked up to see the girl in the tight jeans falling towards him. Her head struck him full in the chest. An electric pain flashed through his whole body, causing his arms and legs to twitch violently. He could not see Mary. His view was blocked by the girl's body. Still the carriage screeched and screamed along on its side. The acrid smell of hot metal and burning rubber assaulted his nostrils. His eyes watered. His head banged repeatedly against something hard. The girl's body bounced on his, almost playfully.

Then just as suddenly, there was silence as the carriage came to a stop. And then the screams started. Trapped under the girl, George listened desperately for the sound of Mary's voice. He did not hear it. He gradually became aware of the pain that was thumping through him. He pushed the girl aside with all his strength, punching and kicking at her to get free. The thumping in his chest became more demanding. He was aware of the dampness of blood on his face and its metallic taste in his mouth. He did not know if it was his or the girl's.

At last, he was free of the girl's weight. She lay, motionless, beside him as he pulled himself up to his feet. Everywhere was glass, luggage, carrier bags and people. People lying, some silent, some screaming, their voices ripping through the dusty air. Above him, the window, now jagged and broken, let in light and, directly above, the clouds looked down, unmoving and unmoved.

He coughed and his mouth filled with blood. He climbed onto the side of the seat to get a better view along the carriage. And there was Mary, lying behind the seat that she had occupied. He braced himself against the side of the carriage and reached for her. As he touched her, her eyelids flickered and her mouth moved. George leaned in towards her.

'Hush, Mary, dear. I'm here.' He slumped down beside her, cradling her. His free hand came to rest on a book. He looked down and saw the author's name. Of course, Jane. Jane Austen. He remembered half-watching the television series of *Pride and Prejudice*, compulsorily silent on Mary's insistence. What was the name of that obnoxious man? The name, Darcy, slipped into his mind as all around him went black.

The sound of voices brought him round. He looked up. His blurred vision made out two faces at the window.

'Here! Help us, for God's sake!' yelled George. The two men shouted to him to protect his face as they knocked out the jagged shards of glass. He leant over Mary. He could see blood dripping onto her clean beige raincoat and realised that it was coming from him. He put his hand to his head and felt tentatively along a gash that ran from his forehead up onto his crown.

'OK, mate, let's have you.' A ladder was eased down. George bent to gather Mary and, calling on all his strength, pulled her up into his arms. Standing upright, he reached up as far as he could. One man came part way down the ladder and caught her shoulders. He pulled as George pushed and Mary was lifted unceremoniously out of the carriage. George hauled himself up the ladder behind her, supporting her body weight as well as he could. Then, with help from the reaching hands, he was up too, standing, swaying on the side of the carriage.

All around he could see dazed and injured people. It seemed wrong, unreal. The long straight track in either direction and the neat suburban streets on each side promised a certainty that had been betrayed. George, his heart pounding, eased himself down another ladder past the filthy oily underside of the carriage. Halfway down, he missed his footing and fell. As he hit the ground, his body jerked inwards as the pain sucked at his remaining strength. He half-rolled, half-staggered down the embankment, coming to a halt leaning against a road sign. He looked up to see a stretcher being gently lowered from the train. An arm in a beige raincoat hanging down from it told him it was Mary. He hauled himself up, leaning on the road sign as she was brought down. He raised an arm and the ambulance men stopped beside him. He looked down. She seemed to be smiling.

'George,' she whispered. He leant closer to her. 'It's you. You are my Darcy. I never… We'll go dancing tonight.' Her eyes lost focus. He sank slowly to his knees. The last thing his eyes saw was the name on the sign. Pemberley Close. Pemberley. Of course. He sighed and closed his eyes.

THE FLOW AND THE EBB OF THE TIDE

On the shore, the waves make crystal patterns at their feet. His thick practical boots are transformed, the encrusted salt shining like jewels against the scuffed black. Beside him, she dances back, afraid the salt water will spoil her sandals.

Aware of his shyness, she looks at him out of the corner of her eye as she pretends to watch the waves. She takes in the hair, tousled by the wind, his jacket woollen, despite the warmth of the day, the trousers stopping just an inch too short above those boots. He glances across at her, for a brief moment returns her gaze before the connection slips away, leaving her with the afterglow of his pale blue eyes, as if she has been looking at a bright light. She shivers slightly and draws her light coat around her, more for protection than warmth.

She discreetly checks her watch. Three hours until the train back. They have successfully lost the rest of the youth club group by wandering out along the beach, away from the arcades and pubs, the Punch and Judy and the donkeys, to the quiet of this cove.

She takes his hand.

'Come on.'

He seems surprised but follows her up the beach to where the rock face rears up. She finds a spot where they are sheltered from three sides.

Late last Saturday night, alone in her room, she had pulled her diary out from under her bed where it lay hidden from her mother's prying eyes. All year its bright, flowery cover had seemed to promise possibilities that were forever just beyond her grasp. She'd perched on the edge of the white candlewick bedspread, diary in her hand. With the pencil from her school bag, she had carefully drawn a line down the centre of one of the blank pages in the back. At the top of one column, she'd put a plus, the other a minus. She'd hesitated then written in the first column. Handsome. Good dancer. Shy. The pencil had hovered over the page and then, with a determined swoop, had scribbled the word. Sexy. She'd looked at that word, felt the colour come to her cheeks. She'd put three carefully rounded exclamation marks after it, as if their childish exuberance could somehow soften the deep, hard threat of the word. It would all have to be rubbed out later, in case her mother did find it. She could imagine having to endure again the hell-fire and brimstone, men only want one thing, get on your knees and pray for purity lecture and the call to the priest, while her father, as usual, sought sanctuary in the potting shed.

And outside that room it was 1965 and the world was turning.

That word, four-letter gateway to something she barely dared to imagine, had smiled back at her. She knew why. She could still feel the sensation of his hands on her from just an hour earlier, on the way home from the church youth club, hidden for a few minutes in the alley behind the shops. Away from the all-seeing stare of Father Robert, she'd felt excited and special. This was the third week he'd walked her home. Each week, she had allowed a little bit more, according to the unwritten rules of these things. She knew what he wanted, and she was beginning to understand what she wanted too. That had come as a shock to her, someone raised on the teaching about a good girl tolerating that sort of thing and keeping it to a bare minimum, and nothing at all before she had snared her man into marriage. But those rough hands carried their own magic, which, even through her jumper and slacks, had changed her skin into a living part of her body.

Under the rock's watchful shelter, the warming sun slanting down, she takes off her coat and, laying it on the sand, sits down. She leans forward, knowing that, from that angle, he can see down her top where it falls forward at the front. After a moment, she squints up at him, making him look quickly away.

'Sit down then.'

He hesitates, then removes his jacket, sets it down with exaggerated care and sits heavily next to her. They look out to sea in silence.

'I like it here. Do you?' she murmurs.

'Aye.'

On Saturday, she hadn't put anything in the minus column for a long time. She was fighting down her mother's unnegotiable and damning two-word condemnation. Working class. Of course there were issues; for one thing, she was going south to university after the summer and he would be staying, working at the foundry. But they could work something out, write to each other. Maybe.

She'd finally written in 'taciturn', a word that she had recently discovered and loved the sound of. It was certainly true; conversations with him rarely lasted long. But the roughness, even the quiet confidence that she felt from him, more than made up for that.

Settled on the sand, she leans into him, puts her head on his shoulder. He glances at her then continues to study the crashing waves. She runs her hand up and down his back.

After a few moments she eases herself away from him and, with a studied poise that belies her nervousness, pulls her t-shirt up and over her head. She reaches behind, unclips her bra and shrugs it off.

She hardly dares to look at him but hears his gasp. She finally glances up. The eyes are wide and more blue than they have ever been. But she's not seeing in them what she hoped to see as he looks wildly round.

He finds his voice.

'What're you doing?'

'What? But, I thought, I mean, you wanted, you'd like to ...'

Her arm goes protectively across her chest.

'No, I mean, yes, I do, I want … But not here. What if someone saw?'

'There's no one around. I did check.' Her voice is catching in her throat.

'You can't be sure, can you?'

She scrabbles to put her clothes back on.

'I just thought, you know, it would be nice …' she mutters.

'Right. And if the Father saw, told your mother? You'd be branded a slag. I'm only thinking of you.'

No you're not, she thinks. If you were thinking of me, you wouldn't give a shit about the priest or anyone. We'd be doing things now that need a thousand Hail Marys. Her language, even in her own head, and the images she was creating, startle her. She feels an excitement flicker, then die, killed by the moment.

She gets up and grabs her coat.

'Come on, we'll be late.'

'We've got hours yet.'

'Just come on. We might get trapped by the tide.'

She looks at the sparkling sea coming in and flowing out and envies its casual ease. Tonight, that diary column will be filled, and in eight weeks she will be at uni and away from all this. Then ... then …

A GOOD NIGHT OUT

I really don't like going out much. Give me a night in with a good tele programme – *Holby City*, football, a clean comedy, not one of these dirty, noisy, unfunny ones that they inflict on us nowadays. Yes, give me that and a small whisky and I'm a happy man. King in my own little castle. But, occasionally, one has to do one's duty. It was the Memsahib's birthday coming up and I was starting to get the 'You don't take me anywhere' speech so I thought that I had better nip it in the bud. A nice meal down at the Beefeater and then back in time for *Newsnight*.

It's ironic, really, looking back, to think what a jolly mood I was in at the start of that evening. I put on my best suit and the wife was looking really pretty good, and I told her so. Always good to hand out the little compliments, I've found. It's only a short drive into town, just down to the bottom of the hill and then off down the dual carriageway, the A424, you know, to the town centre. We were a little late, so I was indulging in a bit of accelerator practice down the straight bit. Suddenly it was all sirens and flashing blue lights. I pulled over and a very tall young policeman unwound himself from the panda car and strode with mighty steps towards me. I pressed the button to lower my window and turned to greet him.

When my nose hit solid glass, it dawned on me that I must have pressed the wrong button. That and the wife saying, rather tartly, I thought, that perhaps, when I had lowered my window, I might also shut hers again as she was getting rather cold. It's quite hard to explain yourself to a policeman while holding a handkerchief to your nose to staunch the flow of blood but he seemed to pick up 'wife… birthday… late' and, with a warning to be more careful in future, he was gone. 'I think I'll drive home,' said the wife. 'Jolly good idea,' said I, trying to make the best of it, 'then I can have an extra glass of wine.'

Safely in the restaurant, we enjoyed a good meal. It's always good at the Beefeater. We had a very pretty waitress too, always a bonus, and I was able to exchange some badinage with her between courses. Perhaps encouraged by a few glasses of wine, I became really quite witty, even a little saucy. Madam was, perhaps, not quite as talkative as usual, though she did seem to enjoy giving me regular updates on the changing colours of my nose.

Our waitress, Sophie, was, judging from frequent whispered conversations, clearly good friends with one of the waiters, a rather surly character, I thought. As the meal finished, I ordered coffee from our little sweetie, though for some reason it was the surly one who brought the tray over. I still don't know what he could possibly have tripped on; suffice to say that a tray full of coffee hit the table and, with the accuracy of a bouncing bomb, plunged into my lap.

I suppose that I should be pleased that the coffee at the Beefeater is never really very hot, but even so I found myself moving more quickly than I had for many a day. Straight into the Gents, whipping the trousers off as I went, rather to the surprise of a man who was already in there, and who seemed to become rather more interested in my undressed state than was strictly necessary, I thought, at that moment. Drawing myself up to my full five foot six, and thereby inadvertently revealing more thigh than was wise in the circumstances, I asked if he could kindly send in the manager. When he had finally torn his eyes away from my lower portions, he scuttled off.

As I waited for the manager, I vaguely remembered some instruction about not letting a stain set, so I soaked my trousers in the basin. I realised ten seconds too late, of course, that this action would now make them completely unwearable.

'No problem, signore' exclaimed the manager, when he eventually arrived, 'I find you a spare pair.'

A few more minutes trying to perfect the art of looking nonchalant while exposing one's naked legs to full view in a Gents lavatory and he was back. 'I'm very sorry, is all we have,' he said, producing a pair of voluminous black and white check chef's trousers. The choice between spending the rest of my life trouserless in a Gents or looking like someone half decided about a career in the circus is not one that I had planned to make that evening but, inevitably, the trousers won. Vastly too big, and held together by a safety pin, they nevertheless covered the necessary area.

I emerged from my bolthole with as much dignity as I could muster which, I confess, was not very much at all and was greatly reduced by the subdued tittering from my fellow diners. The wife has a way of looking at you sometimes – that arch of the eyebrow that seems to combine disbelief, mild amusement and irritation in one small curve. And there it was again.

'I think your coffee's getting cold,' she said, before being swamped by shaking, silent laughter. Having extracted a promise of payment for the dry cleaning, and with the small satisfaction of not leaving a tip, we paid and left. I noticed on the way out that the surly one was now looking decidedly more cheerful.

It was a mild evening and I hit on an idea for drying the trousers. Easing the sunroof back a fraction, I squeezed part of the waistband into the crack, leaving the legs blowing in the breeze. I felt pleased with my creative solution.

True to her word, the wife stepped into the driving seat. She drove back rather flamboyantly. My reminding her of the incident with the policeman did nothing to slow her down; indeed, it seemed to result in greater speed. Given how the evening was developing, I suppose that the next event was inevitable. As we rounded the corner at the bottom of the hill the trousers flew free from the grip of the sunroof and disappeared into the night.

She pulled in and looked at me silently. With a sigh I unfastened the seat belt and climbed out. Although it was now dark, the light of a street lamp was enough for me to realise that the trousers were nowhere to be seen. There was a wall on the far side of the pavement and, guessing that they must have flown over it, I decided to follow them.

Walls are always higher than they look, aren't they, and it took some rather undignified scrabbling for me to get over. I landed on all fours and, staggering to my feet, found myself face to face with six people standing by a barbecue some ten foot away, staring at me in frozen astonishment, hot dogs suspended. With that perfectly timed malevolence of inanimate objects, the safety pin chose that moment to give up its unequal struggle and the black and white check trousers collapsed like a small marquee around my ankles.

I think this is the moment that I probably panicked.

Maybe it was the sight of the man by the barbecue with the chef's hat and the apron bearing the image of an outsized pair of breasts, maybe it was the blood that was now flowing freely again from my nose, the summer breeze round my legs, the dinner wine or just tiredness. Whatever it was, I can share with you that if you ever find yourself standing in a stranger's garden, trouserless, bloodied, with a heavily stained shirt front, it is not a good idea to rub your hands together and enthusiastically exclaim 'Ah, sausages.' As apron man's hand tightened on the wooden mallet, I realised that retreat was the best option. Adrenaline ensured that getting back over the wall was much easier, even without trousers. I landed, again on all fours. 'Hello, again, sir,' said two very long navy blue-trousered legs.

I suppose that it's not surprising that my explanation to the officer was a little garbled, given the circumstances and the realisation that my wife had driven off without me. At least the police car was warm and comfortable, and they gave me a cup of tea and another pair of trousers at the station. It's now three a.m. and I am finally back home, all discussion of illegal entry and indecent exposure now dropped. I don't think I'll go up to bed just yet. A little whisky seems like a very good idea first. And there are some really quite interesting things on the telly at this time of night.

RAIN, SWINGS AND THINGS YOU DON'T TALK ABOUT

She hears him in the hall at twenty past seven, busily putting his coat on. Usual time, usual farewell, 'I'm off to work, dear. See you tonight, normal time.' No kiss, no hug, just a call from the front door.

In the kitchen, she turns up the radio, expels his favourite John Humphreys and that strident girl on the *Today* programme, mourns once again the loss of Terry Wogan and settles for Classic FM as she tidies the dishes.

She makes the beds, hoovers, cleans the loo, singing snatches of *Carmen* and *Porgy and Bess* in a high wavering voice, skimming over the words that she doesn't know. Stops for coffee at eleven, with Ken Bruce's gentle Scottish burr keeping unwelcome thoughts at bay.

At eleven thirty, she puts on her coat and checks her appearance in the hall mirror. A pat to the hair, careful application of lipstick, a tug to straighten out the hem of the coat. Then, with a quick nod of approval, she's in the car, heading for Morrisons. She goes round without talking to anyone, carefully choosing what she chose last week, looking for bargains, pausing before the more exotic vegetables and oriental ready meals before sighing softly and moving on.

She thought of leaving him once, about twenty years ago. No, not about twenty years ago, at ten forty-five on the evening of Wednesday, July 17th 2001. Sitting in George Anderson's Sierra outside the arts centre after her pottery class, holding his surprisingly soft hands. He was off to Spain to open a bar. Would she come? He cried when she eventually said no. That shocked her. But she had responsibilities. She cried once, later, on her own. And wondered. Often. Barry never knew, never noticed.

Lunch is a sandwich in Morrisons, at a seat by the window, looking out at the tarmac of the car park, the usual cheese and tomato, on brown, no mayonnaise, with a copy of *Woman's Own* for company.

It's not that there's anything actually wrong with Barry. Everyone says what good company he is, always bouncy and enthusiastic, a real Tigger. That's what originally attracted her; she thought he would somehow take her out of herself, connect more with other people. Yes, so upbeat, so determinedly, infuriatingly sunny. Bouncy Barry. Grey hairs? Sign of wisdom, bounce. Kids left home? Never mind, more time to ourselves, bounce, bounce. No shared interests and nothing left to say to each other? Ignore it completely, bounce, bounce, bounce.

She delays going back to the empty house, driving on into town. Her route takes her past the arts centre. She wishes it didn't but has never thought to find a detour. She thinks about an article she read in the magazine over lunch. Something about your early fifties being the best time of your life. Fulfilment and freedom, something like that. Free from the kids, as if that's a thing to be desired, as if that's a burden that she wanted to be relieved of, as if she didn't walk round their empty bedrooms every day.

She parks, looks undecidedly up and down the road, then heads for Marks & Spencer's. Stops, hesitant. Rain starts and she hurries into the shop, stands just inside the door, looking at the signs and the corridors of clothing that beckon her in. No. She turns, walks slowly back out, slowly down the road, past her car, on into the park. The rain comes down steadily; people scurry past her.

After a few minutes wandering, she finds herself heading briskly uphill towards the playground, its gaudy colours and metallic shapes an insult to the soft greens of the trees and grass. It's out of place and she likes that. Understands it. Rain smears her hair across her forehead, drips down inside her clean coat collar. She is standing in front of the swings. They sway, gently, enticing. She starts to sway slightly in time with them. She remembers, a life ago, being here with the kids when they were little, the laughter, the energy, being needed.

She looks round furtively. No one. She climbs onto the swing, shuffling herself into place on the tight seat, her coat caught up on the chains. Then, as a memory unstirred for so long forms again, she pushes her body forward and back. Up she goes, higher and higher, driving up through the rain to where she can see the whole world. She laughs out loud. She's singing. Singin' in the Rain, what else? Top of her voice, yelling out the words. She feels complete, connected for the first time for too many years, one with the rain, the sky, the swings and with this moment. Minutes, maybe hours later, she slows down, drops her feet and skids to a stop, breathless.

As she steps off, she slips, tumbles backwards. She lies on the muddy ground, staring up at the rain that falls full on her face. She laughs again, her stomach shaking. Eventually, breathless, gasping, she hauls herself up. Walks slowly back down through the park in the rain, past the silent trees that will keep her secret.

At the car, she removes her mud-smeared coat, folds it carefully inside out and places it on the seat beside her. She must remember to take it to the dry cleaners tomorrow.

Back at the house, she sees herself in the hall mirror, mud-splattered, her hair hanging down in wet strands. A spluttered laugh escapes her, and she's back at the time when she and best friend Susan stole those Mars Bars from Woolworth's. Two fifteen-year-olds giggling behind the lock-up garages, almost sick with the excitement of it all, unable to enjoy their booty.

At her dressing table, a large glass of sherry beside her, she fixes her hair, notices new grey wisps, the lines on her face. Then goes down to prepare supper.

At six thirty-seven, the door slams.

'Hello, dear,' he bounces into the kitchen. 'That smells good. What is it?'

'Chicken casserole; it's Wednesday.'

'Lovely.' He picks up the *Radio Times* and flicks through, 'How was your day?'

'Oh, you know, same old things.'

And, deep inside her, the memory flickers and glows gently, a fire waiting to be coaxed into life.

THE SCULPTOR

I am a sculptor. I forge metal and carve stone and give it life. And today I shall die.

I have always loved objects, things that I can handle and shape. As a child, I can remember picking up stones in the street and seeing shapes and patterns in them, stroking a branch of the olive tree in our garden to rejoice in the complexity of its bark. From the days when I was a young apprentice, I knew that I had a remarkable talent. When I was sixteen, I showed one of my early pieces to the Masters at the Academy in Alexandria. The room fell silent and I could see in their eyes the mixture of amazement and jealousy that I would later come to expect. By twenty-five, I was head of my own academy and master of a thriving studio. People travelled from all over the known world to learn from me.

I was proud of my fame. My studio grew, producing everything from vases to giant statues, all of them carrying my mark. I made my clients feel important and valued.

'Oh, yes, as you see, it's an original Joseph. Well, one can afford the best.'

'A statue by Joseph? Yes, I think that would be a very suitable tribute to my work for this city.'

But always, I kept control. No one told me what to create. I had to accept that some irritating words of self-aggrandisement be carved onto the plinth, perhaps, but that was all. Why do people feel the need to explain in words what I do so much better in form?

I was rich. My home was spacious, many would say luxurious, with large cool rooms looking onto an inner courtyard full of the colours and scents of lemon trees, oleander and hibiscus. Sharp shadows formed ever-changing patterns on the terracotta walls and, more wonderful than anything, the rooms rang with the laughter and shouts of my children.

But I was rarely home before nine in the evening. Mine is not a job with regular hours. When I am inspired, when the stone is talking to me and guiding me, time is meaningless and I would work for thirty hours without pause. When I was not working on a piece, I was being wined and dined by those who wanted favours from me. 'Oh, by the way, Joseph, would you be able to sprinkle a little of your magic on this modest project of ours. We don't have a lot of money, but…' The answer was nearly always no.

They say that no man dies feeling that he should have spent more time at work. How many times have I wished that I had returned earlier to my family, my beautiful, amazing, lost family. I die alone. Perhaps that is right.

The soldiers came in late summer. Our citizens decided to greet them as friends. We let them in to the city, fed them and hoped that all would be well. Then the killing started. No one knows who struck first, only that the King announced that for each one of his army that was killed, a hundred of our people would die. Within days the city was on fire. I stayed in my house on the outskirts, watching, waiting.

The day that they came to my house had been bright and clear. It was early evening but I could still see for miles across the barren land to the hills beyond. So I saw them coming, the dust from their horses' hooves forming a blood-red cloud that cut off the city. Men on horses and camels, faces swathed against the desert dust, some in armour, some wearing the same loose white robes as me. All armed. The King himself led the column, a giant with a broad, flat face and eyes narrowed against the sun and the sand. I called to my family to prepare a greeting. My two daughters carried jugs of water, my son stood ready with wine and my wife was beside me with a plate of sweetmeats.

As they rode through the archway into my courtyard, I stepped forward to bow a greeting.

'I have heard of your skill, Joseph,' said the King. 'You are a remarkable man.'

'Your Majesty is too kind. I too have heard of your prowess. You are the greatest general of our times and I am privileged to receive you here.'

The King laughed. I felt reassured.

'This man knows how to flatter,' he said to his troops. 'Listen and learn, you coarse rabble. Now, Joseph, I have plans for you. Tonight we leave this miserable place. We have all that we came for. And you will come too.'

'Sire, you are kind, and I am honoured, but my life is here, my work and my family are here. Please tell me what you want, and I will complete it in my studio and send it to you.'

The King's eyes were cold. 'What I want, Joseph,' he said quietly, 'is to give you the greatest honour of your life. And you will take this honour. We are going, now, and you are coming with us. And, just to ensure that you understand that your life, as you call it, is no longer here…' He signalled to the troops with him, who rode forward instantly. They moved very fast and were everywhere. By the time I understood, it was already too late. 'Run,' I shouted, uselessly. My eyes, so used to controlling what they saw, took in the horror in panicked flashes. Swords swung down, catching the red rays of the sun, and came up redder. Screams were cut jaggedly short. Blood and wine drained away into the rich earth. Within a minute I stood alone, totally alone, in my now silent courtyard, unable to move as flames rose from my home. My life crumbled through my fingers like the sands all around me. A heavy blow struck the back of my head and I fell gratefully into oblivion.

I remember little of the next days, only the pain. As I jolted across the desert in a blacked-out waggon, the voices and faces of my family came to me talking and laughing, more real than my solitude, welcome and terrifying. I wept, begging them to go, begging them to stay. Over the month that it took us to travel, they gradually receded and each day I was forced to feel the reality of their loss more desperately.

Finally, we arrived at the Kingdom. My hatred for the King did not prevent me from being amazed and impressed. Here in the middle of the desert he had created a fortified city. Inside the walls, paved streets were flanked by magnificent palaces. Wherever I looked, there were gardens and fountains, minarets rose to the sky, markets bustled with life. Half of the space was given over to farming, to ensure that this oasis town could live forever. I had never believed that anything like this could exist. My artist's eye took in everything and saw that it was all of the finest materials, the finest but not the best design. I knew that I could do better.

I was installed in luxurious quarters and the King ordered that I should be given everything that I wanted. But I only wanted one thing and no man could give that. For days I sat looking out on this extraordinary city. Its undeniable beauty began to pall. I could not reconcile the magnificence with such inhumanity. I felt nauseous, smothered by a mountain of over-sweet confections.

Eventually, the King sent for me. I stood before him in his vast marble chamber but this time I did not bow. As a soldier came forward to knock me to the ground, the King raised a restraining hand.

'We must respect a great man,' he said with a thin smile. 'Now, Joseph, I hope that you have been well looked after.' I said nothing. 'This is what you will do,' he continued, showing no interest in my silence. I want a statue. Not just an ordinary statue. I have many of those. Not just a great one, but the biggest, most magnificent and impressive that the world has ever seen.' His narrow eyes fixed me. 'And you, Joseph, are the only man in the world who can do this. You will have everything that you desire, any materials, no matter where from, no matter what price.'

I could have refused. Right there I could have spat in his face and ended it. But I am an artist and already something inside me was stirring, an energy and desire that shamed me but could not be ignored.

For the last two years I have immersed myself in the task. Granite, marble, gold, cedar wood – everything I asked for was brought to me. A great new central square was created, and I worked there day and night, hidden behind high wooden walls. I knew that this would be my greatest work and I was certain that it would be my last. Each day I worked until exhaustion floored me, my obsession blocking out at least some of the desolation that never left me.

And now it is the day that the statue will be revealed. The King has declared a public holiday, but everyone knows their duty and will attend. I made sure that I kept full control over the seating for the great unveiling. The setting is magnificent. The statue soars high above us all, covered in a vast cloth of many colours, tied down by ropes. Tiers of seats surround it; two thousand people will watch it be revealed. The King will be positioned right in front of the statue on a high dais, seated on a gold throne, swathed in purple silk. In my country, purple is the colour of death.

Only I know what will happen. As the ropes of the giant cloth are pulled, the statue will break. I have put fault lines in, just above the knee, where the granite meets the gold, and wrapped the ropes around them. Two hundred tons of stone, metal and wood will fall directly onto the King. And I know that this will not only be the death of the King. This whole city, his creation, is finished. It will crumble back into the dust of the desert and be forgotten.

Now I stand beside the King and wait. He smiles at me. I know that he is planning to kill me tonight, so that I can never create anything greater. He will not have that chance; he will not need to. A hundred trumpets sound. The King gives the order. I move even closer to him, so that I can be sure that my creation and I will die together. As I wait to rejoin my beloved family, the moment that I have longed for, I gaze at the inscription, visible on the base beneath the cloth. Words dictated by the King himself.

My name is Ozymandias, King of Kings
Look on my works, ye mighty, and despair.

MIDNIGHT

They meet at midnight, the soldier and the girl. No bells chime for them, just the soft damp thud of the creeping mortars and the sharp twig crack of the sniper's gun.

He, far from home, far from the shouts and jokes of the Friday bar. She, in the street where she skipped and played with friends now dead.

Stumbling over rubble, bricks that had, until two weeks ago, been houses of warmth and laughter, they reach the shed. No flower-strewn four-poster awaits, just a mattress on the floor, stinking of damp and dogs. An exhausted softness, but enough for a few moments' shelter from the jagged edges of life.

In the freezing air, their breath makes clouds like smoke from a gun barrel. No word is spoken, no gentle seduction, as fumbling hands reach and burrow. Yearning for the warmth of another's body drives them through half-shed clothing to a desperate animal rutting. It is soon over.

He buries his head in the mattress. She looks out through the broken window at the starless blackness. A snatch of violin music comes into her head, learned at Madame's one year ago. Her fingers move against the grubby edge of the mattress, echoing the notes.

Soon, he will promise to return for her, and she will try to believe him.

PRINCESS

On the third morning after her glorious day, it started to rain. Nicola pulled aside the tasselled curtains and stared out of the window. People were scurrying along the Rialto, heads down, where yesterday they had wandered, taken in the sights, stopped for a coffee.

Behind her, she heard Dan emerge from the bathroom.

'Hi babes, what you looking at?'

She didn't answer.

'Much better view in here.'

She knew she had to turn round, knew what to expect. Sure enough, he was standing naked and wet, arms out like Mo Farah at the end of a race.

'You're dripping on the carpet.'

'So, not our carpet.'

'The maid will have to clear it up.'

'For what I'm paying, they should be laying a new carpet every bloody day, I reckon. Anyway, what about it? Want to ravish me?'

'I think we had plenty of that last night, thank you very much. And the night before. Anyway, it's breakfast time. We don't want to miss it.' She forced a smile. 'Need to keep your strength up.'

Dan's smile wavered briefly then, with a shrug and a cheery 'OK, babes', he disappeared back into the bathroom.

Nicola looked around the room at the canopied bed, the rich reds and golds, the dark oil paintings of plump naked nymphs being chased by strange creatures. 'A room fit for a princess', Dan had announced as they'd entered. And it was. Or should have been. Trouble was, she didn't feel like a princess, not anymore.

She had been. On Saturday. Now, as she had many times in the last three days, she tried to remember every detail of the day, her special, glorious day, the day that she had dreamt of and planned for as long as she could remember. The big moments were as clear as a Hollywood movie; her walk down the aisle; the first dance; throwing the bouquet – really irritating that it was caught by that Linda Barber. But the rest was becoming a blur. She felt the panic build. She wanted to recall every compliment, about the day, the place and especially about her dress and how beautiful she looked. Maybe it would be better when the video and the photos came through.

Dan came back into the room, dressed, she was relieved to see.

'OK, babes, let's see if they do a fry-up.'

Venice in the rain did not offer much to them. They bought an umbrella, Dan complaining loudly about the price, and they wandered through the narrow streets, window-shopping and occasionally venturing into the small boutiques. Nicola bridled at the haughtiness of the assistants, the clear assumption that they would not spend anything. She eventually insisted on buying a pair of shoes that she knew she could get for half the price in England. Dan was not pleased.

'That blows this evening's big meal out,' he muttered. 'Spag bol again, then.'

'Got to have a souvenir, Danny. I'll wear them tonight, look like a princess for you.'

'Only if it stops raining. No way you're getting those wet.'

They walked back in silence, holding hands loosely, bought a couple of rolls in a small supermarket and some beers for Dan and smuggled them back up into their room for lunch.

Nicola decided that a bout of lovemaking after the sandwiches would recompense Dan for the shoes, but she kept it as brief as possible. As soon as it was over, she jumped out of bed and went to the bathroom to tidy herself up. When she came back in, Dan had turned on the television. She could see that a football match was about to start.

'Come on,' she chivvied. 'Rain's stopped. Let's go and explore, take one of those ferries somewhere.'

'But Juventus are playing. Can't we just stay in and watch? Go out later?'

'Dan, I did not come to Venice to watch tele. Come on.'

'You go. You've got a bit of a mood on you today and the fresh air may do you good. We can meet up here at about five. How's that?'

Nicola weighed up the idea of walking about a foreign place on her own and the prospect of a couple of hours without Dan. She gave him her best smile.

'OK. I promise not to buy anything. Well, nothing too expensive.'

'You watch out for those Italians. All hands, they are.'

Nicola grabbed her bag, gave him a kiss that, she could see, surprised Dan with its warmth, and, slipping on her new shoes, headed for the door.

As she walked out, her mood lifted. This place, with its towers, arcades and sweeping squares, now sparkling in the sunshine, just made her feel instantly special. As she walked by the water, being bowed to and greeted by waiters, pedlars and boat owners, she was the centre of attention in her own magical kingdom. Gone were the uncaring check-in clerks and security men of the airport, the bored air stewardesses who had so spoiled her mood on the flight out.

She felt a sudden hand loop through her arm and spun round. A girl was facing her, dressed all in silver, her full, medieval robe sweeping down to the ground. Over her face was an expressionless pure white mask with red, painted lips and eyeholes through which gazed two intense pale blue eyes.

Nicola jumped back with a squeak. The figure put two hands to her mouth, echoing, almost mocking, Nicola's response, and bowed her head slightly in a show of apology. She then straightened up and seemed to wait for a further response. Nicola took another step back and collided with someone behind her. Again, she spun round. This time, she was facing a tall man in a long black frock coat. Silver thread glittered along the length of it. Again, masked but this time, at least, the mask only covered the top part of his face, framed by a long silver wig. He bowed.

'Forgive us, Principessa, if we have startled you,' the rich deep voice flowed into Nicola's brain like champagne. 'We could not ignore the beauty of such a one as you.'

'Princ … Principessa,' stuttered Nicola. 'Does that mean …'

The tall man bowed again.

'Si. Princess, for that is what you are, yes?'

'I … well, I …'

'Come, princess, come with us. Let us show you the special moments of this city of magic. Let us be your servants.'

'How much, I mean, what do you charge?'

The man threw up his hands, affronted.

'Principessa, we are citizens of Venezia. We only want to show you our glorious city. It is our pleasure.'

The girl in silver had moved round to stand beside the tall man, a silent presence, inclined slightly towards her, one arm across her chest, the other stretched forward. To Nicola, a reassuring gesture.

She looked around. There were plenty of people. It seemed safe enough. And it would give her a story to tell Dan this evening, when the conversation became slow. And she would be treated like a princess.

'Well, all right. Thank you, I would like that.'

The masked couple each linked arms with her and she felt herself escorted down the Rialto. After a few swift paces, they swung into a narrow alley away from the Grand Canal and the tourists.

'So, Principessa, you are here for the first time in Venezia?' The tall man leant into her as they walked.

'Er, yes. On my honeymoon, actually.' Nicola raised her hand to show the ring that still felt awkward on her finger.

'Ah!' the man exclaimed as the masked girl threw up her hands in delight. 'But what a perfect place to come for a honeymoon! There is nowhere in the world that is so beautiful, so mystical, so…' his voice dropped to a whisper, 'so erotic as this city. But where is your husband? How could he leave such a beautiful girl to walk alone?'

'Why,' Nicola asked, nervous for the first time. 'Is it dangerous?'

'But no! I only mean that a beautiful girl on her own will make all the young men so distracted they will fall in the canals. And the canals are very deep.'

The tight smile under his mask showed Nicola that the man was older than she had at first thought. She found she was telling her two masked companions more and more about herself as they walked, about the wonderful wedding, the rather hollow feeling that she was now experiencing, about Dan preferring to watch the football. She even talked about her father, how he had been the first to call her his 'beautiful little princess' as she sat on his knee. She hadn't spoken about him for a long time and even now did not tell the whole story. She had told no one the whole story.

The alleyway that they were walking along opened into a small square, the darkness giving way to bright light that dazzled Nicola for a moment. As her vision cleared, she could see, standing on the cobbles around her, some twenty or more people also dressed in medieval costume, all masked. There were noblemen and women, harlequins, courtesans and clowns and they all stood, silent and immobile, as a few tourists moved among them, taking photographs. Splendid in gold and silver, scarlet and purple, the figures were gathered in front of a small church in the far corner of the square. Nicola felt as if she had walked into a jewellery box.

The man stopped and directed Nicola's gaze towards an elegantly detailed building, glistening in the sun.

'Here, Principessa, this is what I want to show you. This is the Palazzo Gamboni. Come, we go in.'

'Is that allowed?'

'To a Venetian, everything is allowed.'

They swept in and Nicola found herself in the most beautiful room that she had ever seen. The floor was of white marble, the walls painted so that cherubs and angels seemed to swirl about her head. On the ceiling was a glorious sun, whose golden rays reached every corner. Even as she looked around in amazement, she had a faint sensation that she had been here before, that she knew what would be behind the doors that led off this room.

The tall man spoke softly, so that she had to lean in to hear him.

'In this palazzo lived a very beautiful princess, Donna Amelia Nicoletta. You see, she had a name very like your own. She was famous through all the city for her charm and her beauty and she was very much in love. But he was a young man of less noble birth and her father did not approve. You know how it can be with fathers, Principessa,' Nicola could feel the intensity of his gaze through the mask. 'How they do not always do good things to their daughters?'

Nicola nodded, feeling a lump come to her throat. How could he know? Even her mother, even the police did not know.

'Well,' the man softly continued, 'her father forbade her to marry her lover. He insisted that she marry for money, to a wealthy merchant many years older than her. The poor girl tried everything but without success. The day of her marriage approached. In desperation, she plotted with her lover to escape.'

He paused, staring out of the high ornate windows.

'What happened?' breathed Nicola.

'Come.' His gloved hand reached out and took hers. He almost ran from the house, dragging her across the square to the church. Nicola's new shoes bit into her feet.

They entered through a low door into the darkness of the interior. Around the walls, Nicola could make out gloomy, heavy-framed paintings, images of suffering and martyrdom. A few candles burned at the altar.

'The beautiful princess allowed herself to be dressed in the finest clothing and jewels. She crossed the square on the arm of her father, eyes lowered but full of hope. Her plan was to escape from the back of the church, where her lover would be waiting with two horses. In they came, father and daughter, through that door. She could see ahead, the husband chosen for her, the old man, waiting at the altar, with all the finest people of Venice in attendance.'

He stood silent, arm outstretched, pointing at the altar, glimmering at the far end of the dark nave. A terrible sense of panic, of certainty at what was about to happen began to seep through Nicola.

'When they entered the church, instead of going to the altar, her father dragged her to this side chapel.'

She was pulled towards a narrow opening in the side wall.

'Inside, on the small altar that you see there, lay the crushed and broken body of her lover.'

As Nicola stared, she saw in her mind's eye the lifeless shape, saw the arm dangling down, the blood oozing and dripping.

'The poor girl allowed herself to be led to the altar but, as soon as she was there, she pulled a dagger from her sleeve and, in the swiftest of movements, stabbed first her father and then herself through the heart. And so, my beautiful little princess, the story ends.'

Nicola broke away from his grasp. She longed, more than anything, to be back in the hotel room with Dan, back in the light. She turned towards the door. Immediately behind her was the silent girl who had walked with them. Only now, the white mask was gone, replaced by black. The figure stood, arms out, head to one side. Behind her, in a half circle, silent, stood all of the costumed figures from the square. All now wore black cloaks.

She tried to move but felt a weight, as if of heavy clothing, pulling at her shoulders, holding back her legs. In that moment, she knew with absolute certainty that she would not leave that place.

Half a mile away, Dan sat in the elegant bedroom and cheered as Juventus scored. He helped himself to another beer.

THE DAILY SUDOKU

'Your coffee's getting cold, Mrs Jones. Shall I get you another one?'

She looks up into the round, blank face of the girl, whose name she can never remember. She can recognise in her awkwardness the usual ruse by that rather common manager to get rid of her before the lunchtime rush.

No one calls her Susan any more, just Mrs Jones. Except her father, of course, but he makes it sound like a swear word.

'No, thank you. I've nearly finished my Sudoku, then I'll be off.'

Why do people always want to rush you, she thinks. Don't they understand how long a day is?

She glances up from her paper and smiles with a little tilt of the head at the manager hovering behind the counter. Let him know who is the customer and who is the servant. Very like a giraffe, she thinks, with that long neck. She returns to the Sudoku. A particularly hard one this morning but that pleases her. She is happy to spend the time and to confirm that her mind is as sharp as ever. Little opportunity for conversation nowadays, so one gets one's stimulus where one can.

'You always treat conversation as a competition, Sue.' Don's eternal complaint comes back to her. He usually said it when he knew she was winning, she thinks, with the smallest of smiles. She'd tried to explain. A schoolmaster father, always setting her against her sister, switching his love like a spotlight from one to the other, depending on who had the better marks, who won the debates round the dinner table. But Don, the dreamy son of a dreamy father, would just smile, mutter something about there being an infinite reservoir of compliments, so why fight. He just didn't understand.

Ah, eight in the top right-hand box. That should open up some options.

She looks out of the café window. The early rain has moved on and an unenthusiastic sun is seeping through. Good, chance of a walk over to the park before heading back. Probably full of screaming children but at least it is a noise; better than the silent house with just the disembodied heartiness of the radio. And the afternoon plays are such rubbish, and she has to stick to the rule of not having the television on before six.

She stirs her coffee, though she takes no sugar, and sips cautiously. Stone cold but drinkable. Probably better cold than hot, truth be told. Cold, she can pretend it's some other kind of drink; hot, it's just bad coffee.

Three over on the left there. That should get that side moving a bit.

There are better cafés, of course, but one has to watch the pennies.

The manager is whistling. Don was a hummer rather than a whistler.

'Will you stop that infernal noise, Don?'

'Sorry?'

'That humming.'

'Was I humming? Sorry, didn't realise. What was I humming?'

'It sounded vaguely like 'Land of Hope and Glory'. God knows why.'

'Really? How interesting. I wonder what put that in my head.'

And he'd wander off and she'd hear the humming start up again like an itch.

He was always so bloody happy, she realised. No wonder she was irritated by him.

Two children burst into the café like swirls of gritty wind, shouting to each other. She ignores them. She's often thought that if children were fitted with volume controls, a small knob on the back of their heads that she could turn down, she might have been more willing. She knew Don would have loved to have had children but, as ever, she'd been able to persuade him, explaining the importance of her career, disguising her fear. Encouraged him to get involved in the Scouts. She never explained her need to starve her father of further experimental material for his mind games. She wonders now, of course, in the circumstances, but what's done is done.

She will have to go and visit Dad later. Be told where she's gone wrong. Maybe tomorrow.

Seven bottom right, which means a five beside it. There, that square's finished.

The café is starting to fill up as people come in for lunch. She recognises a few by sight but does not greet them. They probably don't notice her anyway; middle-aged women are always invisible. Well, she will not be hurried; she's paid for her coffee and is entitled to sit here. Nearly finished, anyway, just a few more gaps to fill.

With Don it was crosswords. He'd sit in the high-backed wing chair, clicking his biro, and humming, of course, always humming. He'd toss over a few anagrams, knowing that she liked the challenge. She would triumphantly call back the answer in a tone of voice that implied that it was obvious and why hadn't he got that straight away?

It was only now that he was gone that she'd realised that his quiet smiles and lack of response were as much a strategy as her father's manipulations.

'It's like trying to fight a blancmange, arguing with you,' she'd complained, more than once, and each time the smile and the shrug.

She'd tried to make a big scandal out of his going. Running off with the disgustingly fecund Guide Leader, what a cliché. She'd put out the word on the dreadful woman, of course; corrupting youth, shouldn't be trusted. But she soon realised that being popular transcended logical argument. That was a shock. She couldn't understand how people could ignore her well-reasoned case just because someone was nice. God, what a bland word, nice. No way to live your life, just being sweet and nice to people.

And now, the job was gone too.

'Sorry, Mrs Jones, but government cuts. You know how it is. I'm sure you understand.'

She didn't, she doesn't. If fact, she seems to understand less than ever. All her careful structures are just so much rubble.

She looks down at her puzzle. Something's wrong. Then she sees it. Two sixes in the second row up.

With a sigh, she carefully folds the newspaper, tucks it neatly into her bag and leaves the café.

PLUM

It was the best of times, the very best of times. A Levels behind me, university just a shimmer on the horizon. Time to travel. Time to become me, to give shape to the formless clay of youth. I booked my ticket to New York and the Greyhound bus pass and packed my bags. Three months ahead of travel, adventure and who knows what. American girls had a reputation; the Beach Boys filled my head with possibilities.

There were enough safety nets, friends of my parents, contacts through school to ensure that this was, in reality, a well-structured adventure but I did not let that get in the way of my image as the Last Cowboy of the Blacktop. I had read Kerouac, well, bits of him.

And so, I said farewell to the old life, leaving net-curtained civility for the untamed new country. Strange how this old hidebound world started to feel very comfortable as the departure date loomed. I was not so independent as to refuse a packed lunch from my mother. After all, as I reasoned, she needed to feel that she still had a role. My old BOAC shoulder bag, carried for years in the pretence that I was a well-travelled man of the world, was now filled to overflowing with sandwiches, biscuits, chocolate and fruit.

The airport was a vast chamber of lost souls, wandering slowly between check-in, shops and the very few seats. After a few false starts I checked in the one bag that carried my clothes for the next three months and waited. Already, half of the packed lunch was gone. I joined the slow wanderers, filling the hour until boarding with a sort of glassy-eyed slow-motion rounders between the coffee machine, the book stall and the always occupied seats, with occasional detours to the Gents.

Then a delay of forty-five minutes. What is it about delays that prevents anyone from taking advantage of the extra time? Rather than seizing on the gift of forty-five minutes to do something, we all try to stretch what we would have done in the last five minutes of waiting across nine times that length of time. And, when all that I was doing was wandering aimlessly round an airport lounge, that could become virtually catatonic. Which is why I nearly missed the plane. I looked up to see Last Call flashing brightly against my flight number and scurried along the endless corridors towards the distant gate. No time for those deep thoughts about leaving the land of my birth that I had so carefully prepared. I cannoned down the gangway to the plane, only to slam into the back of a queue still waiting to board. Feeling rather cheated and aware that my gasping for breath was starting to unsettle those in front of me, I checked six pockets, finally found my boarding pass and waited my turn.

Being last on carries a penalty. All of the overhead bins were full. A glare round to see who had filled mine with seven carrier bags was met by serried ranks of tops of heads as my fellow passengers found something very interesting to look at elsewhere. I had reserved a window seat, eager to catch a glimpse of the fabled Manhattan skyline at the first opportunity. I had not, however, allowed for my neighbour to be a nineteen-stone Finnish man who exuberantly overflowed his allotted space. I waited as he struggled out, like a whale trying to get out of a Mini, to let me reach my seat. I climbed in, stuffing my bag down into the footwell. There was just enough space for my feet beside the bag and my companion ensured that my upper body was snugly wedged in.

'Welcome to this BOAC flight to New York,' said a prim voice. 'We hope you will have a comfortable flight.'

Eight hours is enough time to write several chapters of a world-beating novel, to climb the last four hundred feet of Everest and get back, to fry one hundred and sixty eggs, one at a time. Eight hours wedged in a seat by blubber man was, what can I say, rather less satisfying. I perfected a manoeuvre that entailed me flattening my face against the seat in front, twisting sideways and sliding my left arm down to my bag. The first attempt harvested half of an egg sandwich, the other half dropping into my right shoe. Second time, after a rest for twenty minutes until the pain in my back subsided, brought up my Kerouac. I allowed myself to dream of better things.

Then food, or a close approximation, was served. My neighbour gazed with confused disappointment at the small tray of stew and curling lettuce leaf. The stew, brown and shapeless, smelled overwhelmingly of hot plastic but I had been to public school, so was impervious to bad taste and to 99% of all known food poisoning. I ate it quickly, hastened by the hungry looks from the Finn. The stewardesses were clearly unimpressed by Kerouac, which I had left conspicuously on my tray. So was I by this stage. One further contortion after the trays were removed and I replaced it with dear old faithful Wodehouse. Suppressing the feeling that this was hardly New World literature, I happily joined up with the silly asses of the 1920's. The author had, after all, lived in New York for many years.

At last, the Manhattan skyline came into view. No matter how many times you see it on film, there is no match for the excitement of knowing that it is actually there below you. Unfortunately, I would have to wait for several more years before I experienced that excitement as I was sitting on the wrong side of the plane, staring at grey sea.

Moving after compulsory immobility for several hours hurts. It hurts everywhere. I hobbled down the aisle like Quasimodo with piles and it would be twenty-four hours before I became fully vertical again. I was so doubled up that I could barely peep over the counter at passport control, causing the sour-faced controller to check my age several times. Then through to customs.

'Boy.' The voice seemed to rumble from somewhere underground. I looked around, keen to see who was being picked on. 'Yea, boy, you.' The voice, coming from a six foot four black man in a black uniform was clearly directed at me. Why were all the big people picking on me? I did the usual thing of pointing at my chest and raising my eyebrows. Why does everyone do that? As if someone is going to say, 'No, sorry, I didn't mean you. My mistake.'

He beckoned me over with one sweep of his giant arm. I lurched across, eyes fixed on the revolver at his waist.

'Something heavy in that bag, boy? Seems to be weighing you down.'

'Oh, ah, I see. No, you see….' I was about to launch into an explanation of being squashed for eight hours by an oversized person, then thought better of it. 'Just hurt my back a bit, you know.'

'What you got in that shoulder bag?'

'Oh, this? Just the remains of my lunch.'

'Any fruit or vegetables?'

I had read of the need to bribe officials in all of the best American detective stories, but this did seem unambitious, to say the least. And he did not look like a vegetarian. I decided to lighten the situation.

'Well, I might have a plum tucked away.'

His eyes widened from their sleepy, gunslinger style to a wide-awake 'my God, Betsy, they've got Jake' look. He leaned towards me, looking deep into my eyes.

'Son,' he rumbled, 'show me your plum.'

Smiling like a kid cornered in the playground, I reached into the hold-all and drew out a clear plastic bag. In it, instead of a fine Victoria plum, was a coagulated mush. Clearly, Mr Blubber's foot had found it during the journey.

I looked at the plum. He looked at the plum. He looked at me. I looked back at the plum then up at him with my best 'Please don't throw me in jail, mister' expression. A look of great sadness cascaded down the rolls of his face. He slowly shook his head.

'Son,' he sighed. 'I'm gonna have to confiscate your plum.'

After signing five forms confirming that I willingly gave up my plum, that I had no more plums, that I was not trying to invade the United States and that I was not nor ever had been a communist, I was dismissed. I stumbled through the door and into the Land of the Free.

ANTHONY HAWKINS

Anthony Hawkins, stalwart of the church, patient ear to the elderly ladies and loudest laugh in the lunchtime pub, went home, sat down at his kitchen table and wept.

For a week he avoided the mirror in the bathroom, the only one in the house, feeling that perhaps, if he grew a beard, he could somehow keep the world at bay.

Tony Sunshine (his name on pub quiz nights) did not open the curtains, sat in the half-dark, watched daytime television, ate Dairylea and Ritz crackers till they ran out, then tackled the canned fruit left over from the Christmas before last.

After ten days, fearing starvation, he ventured out under cover of twilight, as far as the corner shop.

'Hello, Mr Hawkins,' said Ahmet. 'Not seen you around. Have you been away?'

'In a way,' Anthony replied, went home with his sliced loaf, ham and paracetamol and closed the door behind him.

THE VISITATION

Ann – she dropped the *e* that had originally been attached, seeing it as a symbol of her parents' bourgeois values – is the sort of person you avoid on buses. Though time has bent her, forcing her to forsake many of her favourite vices, she still has a fine armoury to choose from. Tonight, sitting on my sofa, glaring at me, she's majoring in dogmatism.

'Men are already superfluous and will have disappeared as a species within fifty years,' she pronounces with what I would call papal infallibility, were it not for her fervent desire to machine gun the Pope.

Being male, I'm finding it hard not to take this pronouncement personally.

'Don't you think that would be rather dull?' I venture. 'I mean, I've spent many evenings in the company of both men and women, and I do rather feel that the differences are a positive. Seems a good balance of....'

'If by balance,' she interrupts - you rarely get to finish sentences when talking to Ann - 'you mean domination, subservience, stifling of ambition and abuse, then fine.'

'I've never felt particularly dominated.'

I paste on a smile to signal humour. Not good to try being funny when Ann's in full spate. And, on the subject of minefields to avoid, best not to mention the fascination with men that dominated her younger years. Ann's was a life, according to my wife who witnessed it rather too closely, of cosmic indulgence, now visible only in its debris. Those teenage days of flowing hair and fluid morals have marked Ann's face with rivulets of memory, some good, many stained. It all stopped rather suddenly when the nearly pop star boyfriend died, leaving her with two daughters, an empty syringe and the need to get the world in focus for the first time. I keep reminding myself that I should be sympathetic to Ann; she's been through tough times.

Hard though, now that all that past is buried under several years of *New Statesman*, strident conversations, stripped pine flooring and tofu; the latter, to my mind, being a substance best used for filling gaps in the skirting board. Ann does not agree but then Ann does not agree with anything. Anything I say. She sees no need; her every statement is delivered with a wide-eyed certainty that brooks no debate.

'Of course, this government is in league with the Germans. The new Fascists. They are going to take over Europe, just you see. 1933 all over again.'

Ann is glaring at me again. It seems I am somehow responsible for the Fourth Reich, though the two glasses of Chablis, all right, three, that I needed before her arrival have reduced my powers of deduction to a level insufficient to follow her logic. The best equipment for following Ann's logic has always been a weak mind and a spliff and it's many years since I had either.

I let pragmatism intrude.

'I'm going to start cooking. What don't you eat?'

Wrong question. 'What do you eat' would have drawn a shorter answer. By the end of the lecture, which covers topics as diverse as factory farming, European imperialism in Africa, the government adding toxic substances to our food to prevent the inevitable uprising of the proletariat – my fault again, apparently – I realise my cupboard was physically, metaphorically and ethically bare.

I retreat, bloody and bowed. In the hall, I discover my wife, who has been finding essential things to do in every other room in the house.

'She's your friend,' I hiss. 'You go and talk to her.'

'Oh God help me, must I?'

'No point calling on God. She got rid of him years ago. Anyway, you invited her.'

'Did I? I think she just sort of invited herself.'

'Why? She despises everything we stand for.'

'I think it must be a sort of vampire thing. You know, like she needs to top up her despising reservoir.'

'Well, whatever it is, it's your turn. I'm already carrying responsibility for the rise of fascism, the rape of Africa and the horrible deaths of several million chickens.'

She squirms into the sitting room to join Ann like someone who has just failed GCSE Living. I look desperately through the food cupboards to see if we have anything that meets the Great She Wolf's exacting standards. Nothing presents a solution.

I run through the planned menu for this jolly evening. Fish had seemed a good compromise; most vegetarians we know compromise on fish. And on bacon, I've noticed, but that really would be pushing our luck. But it appears that the mere thought of purchasing fish condemns our planet to a mushy doom. The ratatouille is out on its fragrant ear; importing vegetables ticks every box from imperialistic extortion to the destruction of the ozone layer. I wander out onto the terrace for inspiration. And it comes. There, crouching in their plastic tubs, are the potatoes and tomatoes that we have been nurturing all summer.

You don't win with Ann. Any expectation of gratitude or even pleasure is doomed to disappointment. My eulogy to the ecological benefits of growing your own veg are greeted by a grunt. But lack of criticism, I suppose, is a triumph in itself. It may have been the plate of potatoes, steamed in their jackets and tomatoes, fried in oil with herbs from the garden. It is more likely to have been the large amounts of red wine; grapes, it seems, are not an endangered species. Whatever the reason, the grunts, as she devours our votive offerings while lecturing us on the global conspiracy behind cauliflower prices, are received by us with relief and, almost, joy.

The evening wears into night and we sit, anaesthetised by alcohol, nodding gently to the evolving theories, muttering Pavlovian non-committal agreement whenever a pause suggests that this is expected.

Finally, we manage to get Ann to the point where she feels that we have been brought a little closer to her definition of the straight and narrow. We wave her away as she wobbles down the road on her bicycle.

'Do you think she'll be O.K?' asks my wife, reminding me that one of the reasons I love her is her belief in the vulnerability of wild animals.

I pondered the question.

‘Well, she’s just eaten Sainsbury’s potatoes imported from Kenya and tomatoes from Egypt. Perhaps she will wilt with shame.’

‘But I thought …’

‘I never said that they were from the garden. I simply discussed the merits of home-grown food. And I certainly wasn’t going to use up a summer’s work growing the damn things on one evening of feeding the Ever Open Mouth. Now, fancy some fish? I'm starving.'

CRAGGY FACE

‘Have you got your whooshies, love?’

‘Yes, Mum.’

‘Both, the red and the blue?’

‘Yes, Mum.’

Every morning, as he left by the back gate to go to school, his mother would call after him, hoping that, by calling them whooshies, the inhalers in his pocket would somehow become less of an imposition. Blue for regular use in his right pocket, red for emergencies in his left. Though only three ounces or so each, those inhalers weighed him down. But there was another, greater weight.

All his life it had been there, a towering presence casting its shadow over him. At night, when he lay in his bed in the small back room of the house, every morning, as he stepped out into the alley on his way to school, there it was. Its official name on the maps was Addestone Edge, but to everyone in that small mining town, it was Craggy Face. From the backs of the houses, the land rose steeply and, at the top of the hill, jutting out, mocking the town, was a half-mile-wide rampart of rock, forty foot high, fissured and time worn.

Craggy Face was the town’s rite of passage. Although the mine was long-since exhausted, the young lads of the town still had the miners’ stocky build and the need to meet physical challenge. As soon as they could talk, that talk was of the day that they would climb Craggy Face. In the school playground, eyes turned towards the rock and dreams were formed. From the age of eight onwards, boys would come in on a Monday morning with a triumphant ‘I done it’. Parents would greet friends at the corner shop with pride. 'Well, the lad's on his way to being a man.'

But this triumph was shut off to him. More than once, he had tried the climb but had returned breathless, tearful and defeated. Many things made him different; the asthma that had left him on the touchline of boyhood; the academic ability, the shock of uncontrollable blond hair. Young boys are quick to single out the one that does not belong. Man's ancient tribal response was filtered through taunts, kicks and nicknames.

'Could you stop breathing then, Fluffy? I can't concentrate for the noise you're making.'

'Right then Fluffy, is your Ma going to get you some nice ribbons for that hair? Red and blue, to match them inhalers.'

His mother had tried to reassure him as he came back from school yet again with a torn shirt and scattered homework. 'Who cares about that silly old rock? And you've beautiful hair, love. Just wait till you grow up, the girls will love it.' He didn't want to be special. He would pray every night that he would wake up dark-haired and able to run without pain. Every morning dawned with disappointment. He hated the town with its empty streets, its boarded-up shops and its lack of ambition; he hated the boys at school who were happy with what they were, but most of all, he hated Craggy Face.

One June morning, just after his twelfth birthday, two of the girls in his year came proudly into school. They too had conquered Craggy Face. Playtime that day was unbearable.

'So, when are you going to follow the girls up Craggy Face, eh, Fluffy?'

‘I suppose for you it’s a triumph to just get out of your own backyard.’

‘You’re never going to do it, are you, Fluffy? Never ever.’

That Saturday, at six in the morning, he was up, dressed and ready to leave the house. In his bag, he carried a drink, a potted meat sandwich and his two inhalers, the blue and the red. Leaving a note for his mother to say that he would be out all day with friends, he took one last look round the kitchen and headed for the door.

The sun had not yet eased itself over the crag, so he trudged up the slope in the cool of its shadow, looking neither up nor down, left nor right. After an hour, he paused and sat for a while. He could see the town below him, from the river in the west to the silent pithead to the east, all grey in the flat morning light. It seemed deserted, an abandoned film set, the actors gone on to the next show.

Another half hour of walking and he was at the base of the rock. His chest was tight, and his breath forced after the climb, but he did not feel the usual panic of an approaching attack. This time, his body was not going to let him down. This time it was different. The inhalers stayed in his pack. He looked up now. He was at the base of the fissure that offered the most accessible climb. Bottles, cans and plastic bags marked the starting point. Above him, the sun silhouetted the dark top of the crag.

‘It’s just me and you,’ he said aloud. Slinging the bag onto his back, he reached out and put his hand on the waiting rock. Its coolness was surprising and welcome, the next handholds clearly visible. Was his old enemy reaching down to him, willing him to succeed?

'Yes,' he thought, 'it's not me against you, it's me and you, together. We can do this.' Years of anger and hurt coalesced and lifted him off the ground onto the rock. Each handhold appeared with greater clarity, boy and rock with a shared ambition.

After ten feet, the pain in his chest started. He ignored it, climbed on. After twenty feet, the breath was lacerating in and out of his lungs. But still he climbed, seeing nothing but the grey rock in front of him. At thirty feet, his vision blurred, his legs shook, every breath was agony. But the rock was lifting him, forcing him on. It was as if his body belonged to someone or something else. He was without fear, without a past. He could not have stopped even if he had wished to. And he did not wish to. He looked up. The top was close, beckoning him. He reached for the next hold. His foot slipped. His body jerked sideways. The bag swung round, hitting him in the face. The sheer drop opened up below him. His hands and feet scrabbled for a hold. First his hand then his foot found a grip. He pressed his face against the cool of the rock, swore at his own carelessness, at the fickle nature of the rock. But the blow from the bag had cleared his vision. After a moment's pause, he hauled himself upwards.

And then he was there, coming out in the full light of the sun, lying gasping, laughing, staring out at the world below, a world that had moved from grey to full colour. He lay for a full half hour, until the pain subsided, staring at the sky. Then he started back down to a new life.

Later climbers were surprised to see, on the summit of Craggy Face, a small pile of stones and, placed carefully on top, a red inhaler.

MARJORIE'S GARDEN

Marjorie Rawlings really didn't know what to think when her husband Maurice dropped dead one June morning while mowing the back lawn. Her first thought was how cross he would have been that the mower had veered across his neat parallel lines. Then she had to recognise that her overwhelming sense was one of relief. No more would he come back into the kitchen announcing 'Order and structure, Marjorie, order and structure. That's what a garden needs'; no more would he peer into his coffee mug – the one with the Kew Gardens logo – and say 'Bit dark, Marjorie, you do know how I like it'; no more, in the evenings, would he switch programmes from the throne of his armchair without asking her; no more lectures about the iniquities of the 'communist BBC'; no more his thrice-nightly loo visits, accompanied by throat clearing, muttering and door slamming.

Over the next months, though, once everything had been taken care of, Marjorie would look out at the garden with an ever-growing sense of guilt. For years, it had been a geometric perfection, every bush trimmed and structured, every blade of grass of equal height, every fallen leaf swept up and disposed of, no weed allowed to show its head. The grandchildren were forbidden to play on the lawn – 'It's a lawn, not a sports field, mud has no place here' – and even Marjorie was encouraged to view the garden from the solidity of the terrace, rather than risk crushing the grass. Now, wisps of curling shoots were fuzzing the silhouettes of the trees and shrubs, the edges of the lawn were losing their crispness and buttercup had crept in around the pond.

Occasionally, Marjorie would take up the secateurs and snip off some recalcitrant shoots, but her heart was not in it. She felt inadequate. Deciding that she had to get someone in to help her, she placed an advertisement in the shop at the end of her road. For a week, no one answered. Then, on the following Tuesday morning, her phone rang.

'Hello,' said a soft female voice, 'I'm calling about the advertisement. The one for the gardener.'

'Oh, good,' said Marjorie, 'does your husband do that sort of thing?'

'Um, no, I do.' There was an awkward silence. 'I wonder if I might come round to take a look.'

'Yes, yes, of course,' Marjorie stammered, embarrassed at again being caught out by the twenty-first century. 'When would you like to come over?'

'How about tomorrow morning, about eleven?'

'Lovely.'

'Good, I'll see you then. By the way, my name is Eve.'

The following day, the weather broke and the rain came sweeping in. Marjorie gazed out of her kitchen window; the garden seemed to be frowning at her in a reproving way.

'She won't come in this,' she sighed.

Five minutes later, the doorbell rang. Marjorie opened to find a small, pixie-like person with a weather-beaten face smiling at her. She was wearing a scratched and battered Barbour jacket and had a sou'wester pulled down over her head.

'Mrs Rawlings? I'm Eve.'

'Come in, dear. I wasn't sure if you would come.'

'Why not?'

'Well, the weather.'

'Weather has a perfect right to rain.'

'Yes, I suppose it does. Do come in, anyway.'

Eve removed her wellingtons and padded behind Marjorie to the kitchen.

'So,' said Marjorie, looking out of the window at the sodden garden, 'you'll see that it's in need of some attention.'

Eve moved close to the window and looked carefully out. 'Why do you say that?'

'Well, it's not, you know, tidy.'

'Tidy?'

'Well, my husband, my late husband, he liked to, well, keep it, you know, tidy…'

Eve nodded. 'Mind if I go out and take a look?'

'In this? If you're sure. I'll put the kettle on.'

Eve pulled the wellingtons back on and headed out of the kitchen door. Marjorie watched her walk from shrub to shrub, bend down to examine the grass, reach up to run a hand along the branches of the trees. She thought that she could see Eve's mouth moving, as if she were talking to each plant in turn. Marjorie shook her head and got on with making coffee.

After a few minutes, Eve came back, a small puddle forming on the kitchen floor around her.

'Do you know about gardens, Mrs Rawlings?'

'Not really, it was my husband's territory. I'd have quite liked to help but he rather wanted to do it all himself.'

Eve nodded. 'Very green.'

'Sorry?'

'The garden, very green.'

'Well, yes, I suppose… Yes, he quite liked green, my husband, socks, jumpers and so on… Um, coffee?'

'Thank you.'

Eve took the mug and looked very directly at Marjorie.

'Mrs Rawlings, do you know what shrubs you have there?'

'Well, I … no, not really, as I said, Maurice, my husband…'

'Flowering shrubs, Mrs Rawlings, wonderful vibernums, camellias, jasmine, hydrangeas, weigela, honeysuckle.'

'No, I'm sure, I mean, that can't be. I mean, they've never…'

'Keen with the secateurs, your husband?'

'Yes, very.'

'Here's my suggestion, Mrs Rawlings. We do nothing, or, at the most, very little and let nature do what she's good at. We'll just give it a little bit of help now and then; I'll show you how. This time next year, you will have colour, lots of colour.'

'Goodness, that sounds, well, wonderful. But what about the lawn?'

'Do you have grandchildren?'

'Yes, three, all boys.'

'And do they visit?'

'Quite often, yes.'

'So, what you need is a football pitch. Let them run around.'

'But won't that cause damage? And make muddy patches?'

'Yes.'

'Oh.'

'Mrs Rawlings, a garden is a part of you, and you are a part of the garden. Let it bloom and you will bloom.'

Marjorie looked out of the window. The rain was easing. In her mind, she saw the boys running around, tea and squash on a picnic rug below the apple tree, this year bearing fruit, dens tucked into hidden corners, thick blowsy blossoms scattering petals across the terrace.

When Eve had left, Marjorie went into the sitting room. On the bookshelf was a photograph of Maurice, looking smooth and shiny in his best suit. Reaching out, she turned the photo to the wall.

'You'll be happier this way round, dear. You won't want to see this; your order and structure is going to be my Garden of Eden.'

ENGLAND EXPECTS

The soldier sits by the train window, watching the gradually more familiar countryside appear and disappear. He tries to breathe steadily, feeling the air coagulate in his lungs, weighing him down.

For the first three hours of the journey he had sat, huddled, in the centre of the carriage, as far from the windows as possible. Even now, his eyes flicker constantly, identifying dead ground where the snipers might crouch. But this is England; PG Tips and green fields. He is heading for home, that place of certainties where he could be a husband, a friend, the bloke in the pub. But still, no safety, no relief.

He sits back in his seat, feeling the roughness of the fabric against the back of his neck, as reassuring as the coarse blankets that have kept out the cold for so many nights. The countryside blurs as his eyes fill, as they do so many times each day. He is back there.

Sounds fill his head, explosions so powerful that they rip at your stomach, drive the breath from your body. The shouts, baffling, echo through the smoke. Each street corner brings uncaring, random death, no knowing where the bullet comes from as it casually tears bone and brain. And at the end of each day, lying, staring at the wall of a bombed-out house, thinking only that this will all happen again tomorrow.

That day, the day after Jocko and Georgie were caught by the car bomb, he thought about running, had even planned his escape. But where to? In that barren land all the hiding places are already taken. Of course, the hammered-in training kicks him back into action and he stands at the roadblock, scanning the black strip ahead of him. Every curve of the land, every building seem to point at him. 'You're next,' they whisper. *Shout the order, fire into the air, shoot to kill.* The instruction runs through his head like a reassuring lullaby.

When the car comes, it comes from nowhere. Suddenly it is there, already halfway down the road. An old Opel. His Uncle Jack had one, just the same. Maybe it is the same one. Stranger things have happened. The car comes on. Four hundred yards. Three hundred. No sign of slowing. He shouts to the others. 'Incomer. 300 East.' Shout the order, fire into the air, shoot to kill. What is the bloody point? No one can hear you. He crouches. Raises the gun. Two hundred. No change in the engine note. He can just make out the shape of the driver through the haze. Head seems to be turned away. 'What do we do, Sarge?' Pale faces stare at him. 'Fire into the air.' One hundred. No change. 'Shoot to kill.' He is shooting before the words leave his mouth. From both sides of the road, the bullets hit the car. He can see the patterns form on the doors. The windscreen crazes like the frost on his bedroom window when he was a child.

For a moment the car keeps coming. They dive for the sandbags, knowing they are no protection from the blast. He hears whimpering beside him. No blast comes. The car gradually slows. Almost gracefully, it comes to rest against the wall of the house. Silence. They wait for the explosion. Nothing. The rear door of the car bursts open. Without hesitation, the soldier fires. Two others join in. Then he sees. 'Cease fire!' he screams. 'For Christ's sake, stop.' Lying half in the car, half out is a child, a young boy of perhaps seven. The same age as his Darren. His yellow t-shirt carries the cheery logo of a local soft drink. Below him, the red pool spreads.

The soldier runs to the car, ripping open the front door. The sound of singing hits him, the lilting, jolly, unmistakable sound of a nursery rhyme. He leans over the body of the driver, which lies sideways across the seat, wrapped in a heavy coat. He can see though that it is a woman, quite young, her long hair falling free towards the floor. He flicks off the radio. He hears a faint, animal sound. Pulling the woman aside, he sees the face of a young girl, trapped in the well in front of the seat. Her eyes are wide, her mouth open. Her blue dress is spattered red. As he reaches for her, she shrinks back then, silently, the light goes from her eyes.

He steps back out of the car. 'You stupid bitch,' he murmurs. 'You stupid fucking bitch.' He pictures them, singing along to the nursery rhyme, the mother's head turned towards the child, smiles exchanged. He turns away.

'Call HQ. Get them to come and clear up this bloody mess.'

It is all covered up, of course. 'No press, no problem,' as the captain succinctly says.

'You all right, love?' The woman's voice brings him back. Confused, he focuses slowly on the large middle-aged woman sitting opposite, leaning towards him with a look of concern. He can feel that his cheeks are wet.

'Yea, no, I'm fine, er, hay fever.'

The soldier shifts in his seat to avoid her gaze and looks back out of the train window. Fields have given way to factories, retail parks and anonymous, identical houses. He is coming home. Within minutes the train is snuffling its way into the station. End of the line.

Lifting his bag from the rack, the soldier moves towards the door. As soon as the train has stopped, he is out onto the solid platform. In the distance, at the barrier, he can see his wife looking anxiously, trying to spot him, beside her his son and his daughter in a new blue dress. He has longed for this moment, it has kept him alive and now, he feels nothing. Empty. Scared, even, more scared than he has been in the last nine months. He shrinks back, his hand fumbling for the door handle of the train. But then the tyrant training, England Expects, seizes him again and, fixing a smile, he walks forward.

STARLIGHT

'Reckon it's going to be clear tonight, young Billy.'

We'd waited a week for this.

I looked across at Uncle Jake. He was peeping at me over his copy of *Farmers Weekly*, a deeply lined face under the striped bobble hat that never seemed to leave his head, indoors or out. I grinned back.

Through the farmhouse window, I could see the sun setting behind Lacock Hill. The sky around it was a rich, deep blue, streaked with golds and reds, and the light scattered and bounced across the snow-covered fields. Bare trees stood proudly, their branches stretched and still, the deepest black against the sun's final, lingering glow.

For me, even the last few damp, misty days had held a magic in their mystery. Uncle Jake called me 'the little townie' for good reason. The view from my bedroom window at home was of the Chinese take-away opposite and a constant stream of traffic.

'So, what time are we setting out, Uncle Jake?' I liked 'setting out'; it sounded like a real expedition.

''Bout eight, I'd say. It'll be good and dark by then, and we'll have had time for a spot of tea first.'

My Aunt Mary's idea of a spot of tea consisted of a large meat pie with at least three vegetables, piles of potatoes and a freshly made apple crumble to follow, all washed down by mugs of thick, sugary tea.

By seven, we were finished and cleared up. Time crawled by, the way it does when you're longing for something to start. Finally, the minute hand on the old wall clock shuddered towards the top of the hour.

This was going to be the highlight of my stay: a fox hunt, just the two of us. No torches, of course, just the light of the full moon. Not that Uncle Jake was particularly bothered about foxes; he had no chickens, just cows, and foxes stayed clear of them. Hunting was a country tradition, though, and traditions mattered.

We had talked about it for years, at least the five years that I'd spent the school holidays with them, the five years since my Mum had died. 'When you're old enough, young Billy' had been the constant refrain, and this year it was finally happening. I was twelve now and had started to get that feeling that you're part of something bigger, that there's a lot of world out there. This would be a step into that world.

We wrapped up warm; scarf, gloves, extra socks, bobble hat for me too and layers of jumpers topped by a heavy coat. I could hardly move my arms, but I knew how the cold wind, unstopped by buildings, could really cut through you. The last thing I wanted was to have to come home early because I was too cold. That would have been what children did.

Uncle Jake pulled down the long rifle from the wall. I'd been allowed to use it, shooting old cans and stones on the farmyard, but this was different; this was real. He tucked the gun under his arm, and we set off.

'You look after him now, Jacob,' Aunt Mary called from the door.

'Don't you worry, I'll bring him back alive. That's if the fox don't get him,' and he gave me a big nudge with his elbow that nearly sent me flying into the hedge.

We walked out across the rutted farmyard and into the lane that wound down the valley towards the village. The moon was up and so bright that the trees cast their blue-black shadows across the ground. The snow, too, had taken on a bluish glow that intensified in the dips to a cave-like darkness. After a few hundred yards, Uncle Jake guided me through a gate and into one of the meadows. The cows had long ago been brought indoors and there was a stillness as we crunched across the untrodden snow. Uncle Jake touched my arm.

'Stop, lad. Listen and look.'

I stood. The wind had dropped for a minute and I was aware of a silence that, as a townie, I had never known before, a silence like a deep well. I looked up. The sky was full of more stars than I had seen in my life. When Dad had told me that Mum had gone to heaven, I'd imagined her as one of the stars. I was able to look up at night and feel that she was still there. There were a lot of nights when I'd stood at my window when Dad thought I was already asleep. I'd choose which star was Mum and I'd chat to her, telling her about my day. But there were many, many more nights when the city's bright lights and the clouds had hidden her from me. Those were the nights when I felt most alone.

Tonight, though, the sky was packed full, the stars sweeping across in great drifts. It was as if she'd brought all her friends along to watch my special night. There was one really bright star, off to the left and I knew that must be Mum.

I thought about Dad, stuck back in the bright city lights. He was Uncle Jake's younger brother, and the farm could only go to the oldest, so Dad had relocated – dislocated, he calls it – to the city. He always seemed out of place somehow amid the traffic and the noise, like a plant that's been put in the wrong soil. Whenever I got home, he needed every story I could tell about my visit, as if it were a kind of medicine to him. This would be the best story yet.

After a while Uncle Jake and I walked on, trudging up the hill, away from the village towards the woods. Then we heard it. The sharp bark of a fox, challenging and almost sorrowful. Uncle Jake pointed towards the right and, without a word, we headed off that way. By the gate to the next field he paused, his hand on my shoulder. I looked up at him, saw him scanning the open space, those eyes, deep set below billowing eyebrows, almost like an eagle. He nodded and started walking. We skirted the field, staying close to the dry stone wall, me stumbling along to keep up with his stride.

Suddenly, he stopped, crouched down. I did the same and tried to follow his gaze out across the field. It took me a moment to see the dark shape that moved with a bouncing grace a few hundred yards from us. It was heading our way and the moon was at our backs, so gradually I was able to make out the features and even the colour. The field rose from where we crouched, so the stars framed it as it walked, in command of its world, head up, unhurried.

Slowly, Uncle Jake passed me his gun.

'Here you go, lad, it's loaded and ready,' he whispered, his voice as quiet as a rippling stream.

I took it from him, shook off my gloves and slowly eased the gun up to my shoulder. Still the fox came on, walking towards us, until it was only a few yards away.

I squinted down the sight. At that moment, it seemed to sense our presence. It stopped. The head came up even higher. I could see its eyes, gleaming with moonlight. My finger tightened on the cold trigger. Then, behind the fox, almost over its shoulder, the bright star, Mum's star.

The fox didn't move, just stared at me, challenged me, the intruder in its kingdom. I didn't even breathe. Then, I eased my finger off the trigger and, slowly, I lowered the gun.

The fox's head went down, it turned away and trotted off across its field. I handed the gun back to Uncle Jake.

'Sorry…' I muttered, staring down at my feet.

He gently took the gun away from me.

'Don't worry 'bout it, lad. To be honest, I reckon you've done good there. That was a young female, probably foraging for her family. Best to let her be, maybe.'

I knew he didn't mean it, but I was grateful.

The fox was close to the gate now. She turned, took one look back at me, then disappeared.

We walked home in silence, just the crunch of the snow beneath our boots, Uncle Jake's companionable arm across my shoulders. The stars were even more intense now. Mum's star seemed to pulse, as if sending me a silent message. As I watched it, I felt grow within me a great sense of success and fulfilment, something I had never felt before. I knew I had done the right thing and I knew why.

A BOWL OF CHERRIES

There were days on the road when he'd longed for the sun, days when damp clothes hung heavy and he smelt like a stagnant pond. But not this day. A vindictive heat starts to build before ten. Not that he wears a watch nowadays, but he sees the clock on the old church as he walks out along the road of whitewashed buildings.

As the town drifts into countryside, the shade from the high buildings dwindles. For the first few miles, the meandering river flirts with the long straight road as it crosses the valley. Every mile or two, as the water comes close or sweeps under a bridge, he is able to step away from the heat of the tarmac and its dense liquorice smell and clamber down the parched bank to drink and bathe his face. But now, as the road begins to climb, the river turns away and abandons him.

Though his body already carries a deep tan from four months walking, he can feel that tender ache on his face, arms and legs that will become a red pain by nightfall, sensitive even to the touch of a bed sheet, if he is lucky enough to find a bed.

It is at times like this that he feels that his friends might have been right after all. 'You're too used to the soft life, Jack. You don't get room service when you're sleeping under bridges, you know.' Yet, to his surprise, he does not miss the high tech apartment or the restaurants just around the corner where they knew his name and always gave him the same table. That was another person in another time, a time with Mary.

He bends forward, leaning into the hill to prevent the weight of the backpack staggering him back down. The sun seems to chase him into each bend and then be waiting to ambush him as he plods on round the corner. As the road curves upwards round a bare rock that bounces the heat back at him, he stops, the first time in two hours. In front of him the steep hill levels off slightly, winding up through a village. A mean scattering of houses shrinks into the hillside as if searching for shade. Corn, golden and still in the afternoon air, stands in the fields. He can smell its sharp dryness, mixing with the dust to catch at his throat.

At the side of the road a sign, one corner broken off and half hidden by weeds, announces Monte Speranza. 'Hope mountain? I don't think so,' he mutters aloud and walks slowly on. The village is silent, the men no doubt out in the fields, the women sleeping off the exertions of a morning washing, baking and sweeping.

In the centre of the village stands a café, shuttered and silent. Disappointed, he realises how hungry he is. He wipes the sweat off his neck and face with the back of his hand and sits on a large stone by the road to rest, looking down at how the sweat has tangled the hair on his reddened arm. He does not like to rest. When he rests, the thoughts come sneaking back, memories of laughter and lovemaking.

'Sete, signore?' A soft voice behind him breaks into his thoughts. He spins round. A young woman is standing in the shade of a doorway holding a jug of water and a glass. He jumps to his feet, replying easily in Italian, a language he has come to love, that helps him to be someone else.

'Si, molto, signora, grazie.'

She smiles and pours water into the glass. As he walks over, he takes time to look at her. Probably in her early thirties, a good ten years younger than him. Around her eyes the lines are starting to form and in the eyes themselves, despite the smile, an echo of his own sadness. She stands erect, almost defiant. He takes the glass and drinks it down quickly. She motions him to sit at the table on the small uneven terrace. Putting down the jug between them, she joins him in a way that seems almost conspiratorial.

'Have you travelled far?' Always the same question. In the earlier days he would reply 'Not far enough'. But now that the joke has become true, it does not bear repeating.

'This morning, from San Felicio, about twenty kilometres.'

'Only fifteen.'

'Really?' It seemed further.

He waits for the inevitable follow-up.

'And where are you going?'

He shrugs. 'I don't know. Over the hill and we'll see what's there.'

She stands up and goes into the house. He worries that he has offended her. He waits, looking out across the dusty square. The paint on the café door opposite is peeling, exposing wood as deeply grained as a farmer's hands. Dark stains scar the whitewash on the walls, where the winter rains have forced their way through sagging gutters. In the centre of the square a poster, curled at the edges, advertising a circus that passed through the nearby town some two months ago. And above it all the unchanging blue of the sky. Not a bird disturbs its symmetry. Not a sound can be heard. And everywhere, the sour smell of dust.

She reappears with bread, goat's cheese and a bowl of cherries.

'Eat. You must be hungry.'

He stammers his thanks and tears off a piece of bread.

'Aren't you eating?' he asks between bites.

'No.'

'Why are you smiling?'

'I don't know. It's just good to see a man enjoying his food.'

'Doesn't your man enjoy his food then?'

She looks down. A moment of deeper silence.

'My man is dead. Killed last year on the road. Over the hill.'

'I'm sorry.' He wants to say so much, to share memory and loss. But he cannot.

'So, you live alone?' She looks up sharply, suspicion narrowing her eyes. 'I mean,' he stumbles on, 'Do you have a family? Are there people who look after you?'

To his surprise, she leans back and laughs. 'You know very little about Italian life, Englishman. No one looks after a woman of my age. I look after them. Yes, I have two children. They are at the school. And my father-in-law has decided to move in with me. I guess he's hoping for more than just a good meal from me but he's not going to get it.'

He looks up, surprised at her candour. She gazes steadily back at him.

'You are wondering why I'm telling you all this? Because in a few minutes or a few hours you will walk away and never return and that gives me the chance to say the things that I can never say to anyone else. Is that a fair exchange for some food and water? Eat your cherries. They are good. From my own tree.'

He looks down at the bowl of glistening deep red fruit. He reaches in and takes a handful. The sharp sweet flavour explodes in his mouth. The juice runs down his throat and seems to clear all of the dust of the morning in a way that water never can.

‘They’re wonderful.’

‘I know.’

He feels he should repay her candour by telling her about himself. He wants to but cannot think of the words that would unlock the story.

‘And there’s another reason, Englishman.’ She interrupts his thoughts. ‘I believe that you know something of what I have been through. I can see it in your face, in your body. I was watching you coming up the hill. You’re carrying your own personal hell in that backpack, aren’t you?’

For the first time, he looks straight at her, forcing himself to lock onto her eyes. She stares back. The silence lasts a long time. Finally, he looks down.

‘Yes.’ Is that all he can say?

She waits.

‘Yes,’ he continues hesitantly. ‘I have seen what you have seen, felt what you have felt. My wife…’

‘Who is this?’ The voice comes from behind him. The woman stands up, straight-backed and again defiant.

‘He is a hungry traveller. Marco would never turn someone away. In this house, we always look after the traveller.’

The man comes round into Jack’s field of vision. The eyes, permanently narrowed by the force of the sun, are steel grey and glare out of a deeply lined face, marked by a long white scar down one cheek. Jack stands up. The man is short and bent and Jack looks down on him, but there is no question about who is the stronger.

The older man spits a stream of tobacco juice onto the ground. ‘So, traveller, I hope you have not emptied our larder.' The woman begins to speak but he cuts her off. 'What is your name?'

'Jack.'

'Just Jack?'

'That's right.' Back at the place he used to call home there were business cards, name plates, credit cards. Now, Just Jack is so much simpler.

A dry laugh shakes the bent frame. 'Then I am just Giorgio.' He pushes out his hand. Jack takes it, noticing Giorgio immediately look away as they make contact.

'I am driving down to Valdermina in a few minutes, Just Jack. I can take you down there.' The woman, who has been clearing the dishes, stiffens and looks up at Jack. Giorgio's eyes move quickly from her back to him, waiting for the reply.

'Um, thank you but I like to walk.'

'In this heat? You'd be crazy. No, I will take you. I have to get some spare parts. Wait here. I will get the van.'

Jack sits back at the table.

The woman looks down at him. 'You'd better finish the cherries.'

'Do you have more for yourself?'

'No, these are the last but I don't want him to have them.'

He eats them slowly, one by one, savouring each, spitting out the stone. She stands and watches, arms crossed. He cannot look up at her but concentrates on the dwindling pile of cherries. The silence between them somehow seems best unbroken. Within a minute, that silence is destroyed by the raucous coughing of the van's engine. It pulls up beside the table.

Giorgio leans out. 'Get in, Just Jack.' It is not a request.

Jack picks up the backpack and turns to say goodbye to the woman. She is not there. He goes to the door and calls in.

'Thank you, signora. For your hospitality.' No reply comes. He climbs into the van, burning his hand on the hot doorframe.

With a grinding of gears, they are off up the hill. Giorgio sends another stream of tobacco juice out through the open window. 'This place is boring, Just Jack. I show you a bar in Valdermina, plenty of pretty girls.' He attempts a smile. 'They know me there. You will have a good time.' Jack looks out of the side window. The van is unbearably hot and smells of oil, stale tobacco and other things best left unidentified. As Georgio throws it into the first bend, Jack looks back. Behind them, the village of Monte Speranza is silent and empty.

SUMMER WITH ELLIE

'Good sermon, vicar,' I beam as reassuringly as I can, given that I didn't listen past the first two sentences.

The young vicar reaches out hesitantly to take my hand; he's unsure whether he has seen me before.

'Thank you. We all go round to the hall for a post-communion cuppa. Would you like to … um … join us?'

'Perhaps next week.' Dismissive, senior manager voice to avoid further questions. Not knowing whether to continue the conversation, he offers a vague 'We'll look forward to it' to the space beyond my left shoulder and turns to the next in the line, as the queue bunches, impatient for their coffees. 'Ah, Miss Jameson, how's the leg?'

Seeking the sanctuary of my car, I walk down the path, passing the high gravestones and small gossiping groups who toss excluding smiles in my direction.

I lean back into the leather of the seat, closing my eyes. 'Before you were born, young man,' I mutter, 'Before you were born.' Words that I never thought I would use jump, arrogant and unwanted, into my head. How and when did this suited, aging – no, old – BMW-driving body that I inhabit grow out of that wild, free boy? I had hoped that this dark, beautiful, terrible place would give me an answer but, no, there would be no coffee in the hall next week. There would be no next week.

All that summer, we rolled in the sun and splashed in the rain, the drayman's daughter and the vicar's son, swinging high into the hills above the village, running, laughing, touching, whispering sweet obscenities. We owned those days, ours to be squandered.

Funny to think that, for the two years before that, ever since my father and I arrived, Ellie had been the bane of my life. Mocking my Sunday best, scorning my eagerness to learn and excel, mimicking my accent, 'Oh, I say, that's nort fair.' Until the day when, tripped by her outstretched boot, I had ended full face down in the mud, my chorister's cassock and surplice bedraggled and ungodly.

It was as if that incident closed the book for her. The next day, as I made my way cautiously round the puddles down the main street, Ellie called to me from a doorway.

'Simon.'

I carried on walking. 'What?' I called over my shoulder.

'Simon, come here.'

'Why?' I did not stop.

'Come here. I need to talk to you.'

I slowed my step. 'What about? I don't need to hear anything from you.'

'Come here, you daft 'aporth. I want to apologise,' she said abruptly.

I turned to her, wary. 'You can apologise from there, then.'

'Are you going to come here or am I going to have to come and get you?'

I considered the prospect of being dragged across the road by a girl. I walked towards her. As I reached the doorway, she leaned forward, grabbed my lapel and, pulling me in, kissed me full on the lips. I sprang back.

'What was that for?'

She smiled. 'I felt I owed you.'

I could say nothing. I had been kissed before; I was fifteen, after all. It had been by a large girl called Annabel at my cousin's party that previous winter. Clinical, tight-lipped and efficient, nothing like the warm, animal connection that Ellie had just shared with me.

Ellie laughed at my stricken expression. 'Well, that's woken you up. Now what?'

'What do you mean?'

'I mean, what do you want to do? It's summer, the sun's shining, and I bet you're thinking about reading some book somewhere.'

'No.' I felt my face redden; she could read my thoughts.

'Right, you're coming with me. Got any money?'

'Some. I was on my way to the grocer's.'

'Great. Get two pies, some bread rolls and a bar of chocolate and meet me round the back in five minutes.'

'But it's my father's money. He's sent me down to get some eggs and cereal.'

'He can wait. We've places to go.'

For the first time in my life, I ignored my father's instructions. Five minutes later, I was behind the shop, showing Ellie what I had bought.

'Grand,' she said. 'Come on.' And she was off along the lane that led away from the village and up into the hills. I ran to catch up.

'Where are we going?'

'Dunno,' she smiled. 'Somewhere.' After a few minutes climb, she turned off towards a stile. 'Know what these are called, Simon?'

'Stiles?' I replied, confused. Again.

'Kissing gates. Every time you go through one, you have to kiss the person you're with. Ready?' She leaned over to me, eyes closed and lips pursed in a parody of

Hollywood cuteness. I looked nervously in all directions and, seeing no witnesses, put a hand on each shoulder and planted a kiss. I both felt and heard the laughter bubble up inside her.

'You're going to have to do better than that. Come here,' and she pulled me over the stile and down behind the wall. Five minutes later I was five years older and deeply in love.

That evening at dinner, I explained away the absence of eggs to my father. 'I met up with some friends from school and we had a picnic.'

'Well, you should always check with me,' he murmured, returning to his book. I looked through the high windows towards the reddening hills, with their promise of a summer unlike any other.

In my memory, everything of that summer has merged into a kaleidoscope of sounds, sights, sensations. Running through the fields, the long grass caressing our legs. Swimming naked in the high pools, the cold water leaving our bodies tingling after the hot climb. Listening in the soft evening to the sound of nightingales, high above, singing only for us. That summer, I learned to laugh, graduated from the polite smile of my previous life to a shouted outburst of pure happiness, echoing across the valley, bouncing off rocks and returning to me, stronger. And Ellie, always Ellie, running ahead of me, diving and swooping like a young kestrel, one minute in my arms, the next a thousand miles away.

Gradually, but too quickly, the corn filled and stretched out towards the sun. The fields that had been soft became hard and resistant. The smells changed from light, gentle perfumes to the rich, fecund promise of completion. School was starting in two weeks.

It was that Sunday, ten days before the start of term. I had to stay in during the day because of a visiting aunt. 'I'll see you after Evensong,' I'd promised Ellie. The sun was setting as I hurried across the churchyard towards the high street.

'Simon, where you off to in such a hurry?' The voice came from behind one of the biggest gravestones. I turned towards the familiar drawl.

'Ellie, you surprised me.'

'Glad I still can. Come over here. I've another surprise for you.' I walked over. She had spread a blanket behind the gravestone, concealed by its massiveness from the church itself. On the blanket, she had placed a bottle of cider and a bar of chocolate.

'Here? You must be crazy.'

'Why not, we've tried everywhere else. Come on, Mr Prissy. Come and sit down.'

The dark yews that hung over us seemed to gently cradle us, as they deepened the gathering darkness. Half awake, half dreaming, as the cider took its effect, we nestled down. The soft exploring that had become almost familiar, though still magical, was driven that evening by the knowledge of something ending. Close to tears, we held each other in silence. Feeling the cooling air on our skin, we wrapped the rug around us.

'Simon. What on earth are you doing?' I swung round to see the tall figure of my father. 'Into the house at once.' And he stalked off.

Ellie stared at me, eyes wide and shining in the darkness.

'It will be OK,' I whispered. 'I promise.' Ellie nodded silently but I knew, we both knew.

I gathered my things together and walked back to the vicarage. My father was standing in his study, looking out at the night sky.

'I have never seen anything so outrageous,' he said, his voice quiet but shaking. He did not turn but kept his back to me. 'That a son of mine should desecrate God's land in such a foul way. And with that common little slut. Well, I'll soon put a stop to that.'

I should have spoken. I should have told him that Ellie was all I wanted, that she had given me more than he ever could. That I was alive for the first time in my life. But I didn't. I stood, my hands behind my back, staring at the floor and throwing it all away.

A week later, I was on a train, sent to a boarding school on the West Coast of Scotland. Before I returned, my father had transferred to a suburban parish outside Birmingham, all mock-Elizabethan gables and polite gardens.

So, here I am, a lifetime later. Two loveless marriages, three children who don't talk to me, a decent pension, a comfortable BMW and not much else. I never tried to find out about Ellie. This is the first time I have been back. But I'm not going to ask about her, in case someone tells me. The place has changed beyond recognition anyway. Our fields are housing estates; the grocer's is an antique shop. I won't come back. I have no time left anyway.

But I still have Ellie, running, laughing, her red hair streaming out behind her. I still have Ellie.

ELEPHANTS AND BINDWEED

'There was a time,' she said, 'when I had elephants in my back garden. Really.' She looked out of the café window. Half past ten in the morning and still not quite light. The rain was huddling into puddles, the harsh light from Boots and Burger King seeped out into the grey street. Cars splashed by, driven by strangers.

She looked back to the man sitting opposite. His look of concerned interest had become congealed by her long silence. She could think of nothing else that she wanted to say. She took a deep breath.

'In Kenya, you know, where I grew up. But no, you don't know, do you. Why should you? Anyway, the elephants would sometimes break through. One year they ate all Daddy's vegetables. I, er, it was very sad, really, and, um, a little scary, I suppose.' My vegetables, too, she thought. I helped Daddy plant them that year, scraping a trough in the red, sandy soil, counting in the seeds, watering them carefully every day after lessons, breathing in their acrid smell.

'They're your responsibility, Scout,' he'd said. 'Make sure they grow big and strong, like you're going to.' Always that little tingle when he called her Scout. His special name for his special girl. Then the elephants came.

She had been staring into her empty cappuccino cup, watching the brown scum slip slowly down to the bottom. What was she doing here with him? Her car was parked just two streets away. It would be so easy to simply get up, say 'Excuse me, I have to go' and get back to the familiarity of the scuffed driving seat and scattered toys.

Ten years she had been in Britain; ten years in which domesticity had crept around her like the bindweed that had constantly threatened to strangle their crops. The soft rolling Kenyan Highlands of her childhood were now faded to sepia memory; its vivid sunsets, full of colours that could not be named, were crushed by the bland pastels of the damp Home Counties.

'We'll grow more next year,' Daddy had promised. 'There's always next year.' Then a knock on the door one evening. A man's subdued voice in another room as she sat playing with her dolls. Her mother's sudden animal scream. A doll, falling slowly to the floor, lying spread-eagled, face down. She had rushed in to see a neighbour kneeling beside her mother, collapsed in a chair. 'Ambush,' she heard. 'On the north road coming out of town.' And she knew. No one would ever call her Scout again.

Her mother had sold the farm almost immediately. They had moved to the capital, where they both had to learn to be with people. It was hardest for her mother. For fifteen years, all she had needed was the silent companionship of her man. Now it was tea parties, tennis club soirées and concerts to raise funds for the local hospital. An ill-judged loveless affair, quickly defeated by the very loneliness that it sought to soften, closed many doors and her life retreated, without regret, to the two-bedroomed flat and the memories.

But, for her daughter, this was not enough. So, it had been a relief when she escaped to England, away from the unblinking stare of white Nairobi society. She had an address in Chiswick, friends from college who had also escaped. Sleeping on a sofa in their draughty flat, she felt free again. The drabness of the London winter, with its grey lid of cloud, seemed to generate a frantic, defiant indoor life.

Smoky pubs and musty basement flats took the place of Nairobi's manicured lawns, screw-top wine bottles on sticky worktops replaced white-gloved servants. It was at one of these parties that she met John. Twelve years older than her, he was the most sophisticated man that she had ever met and, since her father had been killed, the kindest.

And now she was betraying him. And their children. Planning to head north with a computer salesman who had the beginnings of panic in his eyes.

That night at the party, she had watched John make his entrance. As soon as he had greeted his hostess with a kiss on each cheek, he made his way across the room to stand directly in front of her.

'Now, you were not brought up in this country. No English rose stands as if she is facing a lion. They wilt, you're poised, ready for fight or flight. Tell me.' It was a long way from the usual 'Hey, beautiful, where d'you get the tan?'

'Kenya,' she answered warily.

'Know it well. I was based in a place called Nakuru in the Highlands for two years.'

'Really? We were only about fifty miles from there. We had a farm. What were you doing there?'

'Oh, this and that. I was with one of the NGOs. Helping to build a couple of orphanages.' She could tell immediately that his work had been much more important than he was implying. She could also tell that it was not the conversation that he wanted to have.

'How do you know our hostess?' she ventured.

'I'm much more interested in how I get to know you. We clearly have a lot to talk about.'

'We do?'

'Believe me.'

And they talked. And she talked more, said more than she had for years. They talked on as their hostess tried to persuade them to circulate; they talked after they slipped away for a late supper at a small Italian bistro, where he persuaded her to try vongole sauce for the first time. She told him all about creeping up to the watering holes at dusk, watching lions, crocodiles and rhino. About flamingos turning the sky pink and dancing in formation on the lake. The deep dusky scent of the tobacco drying in the sheds. The sound of the storms beating on the tin roofs. They talked all the way back to his flat until the moment that they fell silent. Then, next morning and all through the weekend, over breakfast, running from the rain, being shushed at the back of the cinema, where even Fellini could not silence them.

Three months later they married in a small church in deepest Surrey, surrounded by the soft awakening of spring. Her mother came over for the wedding. She seemed smaller and she kept people at bay during the reception with a polite smile and a nod. At the airport, as she left, she hugged her daughter awkwardly. 'Well done dear,' she whispered. 'Look after him. Keep him safe.' And for the first time, her daughter felt the beginnings of the bindweed creeping back around her feet.

Two years later Ben was born and Katie eighteen months after him. Now both were at school and she found herself trapped, alone in the rose-covered cottage and high-walled garden that her friends so envied. Whenever John came home, exhausted from another long foreign trip and frustrated by the lack of vision of ill-informed junior ministers, she had nothing to tell him about what she had been doing. She could not even remember. Occasionally she would dress up for fundraising events in London. 'And what do you do?' asked stooping men in grey suits. 'I'm John's wife, isn't that enough?' she'd laugh. It wasn't.

The gym at the local hotel gave her the chance to work off some of her anger. It was there in the bar that she had met the computer salesman, down for a conference that held no interest for him. She was putting off the time when she would have to return to unmade beds and the weekly Waitrose shop.

'Mind if I join you?'

She'd shrugged.

'Been to the gym, I see. Me too. Good to keep in shape, isn't it? You never know when it might be handy.'

An hour later they were in his bed. No momentous decision, it was just easier. There was some physical pleasure in the newness, a younger man who was not tired. But nothing else. No cure.

'I'm going back tomorrow. To Manchester. Want to come? Could be a good laugh.'

She did not know whether it was just post-coital politeness but, when he'd suggested a meeting the following day, she had agreed. Overnight, the children asleep and John away in Asia, the idea of escape grew greater. This man had seen her as herself, not as someone's bolt-on. She could get back to who she really was. No, not get back, it was too late for that, but get away, reinvent herself. No one would understand, of course. Leaving the great man, who so needed her support. That would be condemned as selfish. And the children. A phone call later to a friend to pick them up from school would, at least, be a start. A heavy stone settled on her heart and, she knew, it would never release its grip. The children. Her children. Perhaps they could visit. Perhaps.

She was at the café on time. He was not there. She sat in the corner, her back to the wall, facing the door. She thought about the suitcase, packed in the boot of her car. Five minutes later, in he came, apologising so profusely that she knew he had been watching to see if she would appear.

The coffees were drunk quickly, through stuttered snatches of conversation, thrown like hopeful fishing lines into an empty sea.

'I've got this incredible apartment, you know, in Salford Quays. Prices are rocketing. Really well kitted out. Everything totally digital, underground car park for the motor, even got its own gym. You'll, I mean, you'd like it.'

She put her hand on his. 'It's OK. You can go. I have things I have to do. Thanks.' She looked down, not wanting to see the relief in his face.

After he had gone, she ordered another cappuccino and started to write the list for the delayed Waitrose outing. She stopped and, as tears blotted *baked beans, soap powder*, she signed the bottom of the page, with a flourish.

Scout.

Also by Phil Lawder

The Banker's Ex-Wife

In this comedy mystery for today, a surprise is coming to complacent, unambitious, happily divorced and not very likeable Kate Bradshaw. In fact, a lot of surprises, not many of them pleasant.

It's amazing what you learn when everything is taken away. Pouting Anastasia, possibly sister to the very solid Boris, and the mysterious Muddle open new worlds for her, as Kate discovers who she can really be.

And so, on a journey that takes her through Job Centres, gangsters, casinos, a brothel, street fighting, attempted kidnap and a nice picnic in the Derbyshire hills, Kate gets to understand the world, and herself, a little better.

She may even end up liking herself; you may even end up liking her.

The Old Buggers' Brigade

A contemporary thriller, a dystopia that feels all too possible.

The streets of Britain are no longer safe. Stirred up by ambitious politicians, the younger generation have started to attack the rich oldies.

Jenny is retired, wealthy and bored in a polite suburb of London. She seizes the chance to fight back as part of the Old Buggers' Brigade, and to feel the excitement that she is longing for.

But things are never what they seem, and she is quickly drawn into a world of danger and deception that threatens the lives of her family.

Edges

A collection of poems about the magic of the ordinary, the unspoken undertow of relationships and the quiet desperation of the suburbs, that strange human geometry where edges clash, merge and intersect.

This is a world you will recognise, a world of supermarkets, the weather and random chance. And love – confused, hopeful, frustrated, uncertain love.

ACKNOWLEDGMENTS

My thanks go

- to Siobhan Curham for her editing skills and support
- to Susannah Straughan for her highly professional and knowledgeable proof reading
- to Colin Robinson for his patient and highly creative work on the cover
- to Richard Cutler for his wise advice
- and to all my fellow writers who listened with patience and gave me their views with generosity and constructive support.

Printed in Great Britain
by Amazon

69307787R00073